Ursula's
Yahrtzeit Candle

First published by BCWryter Publishing

First Edition: May 2013
Printed in the United States of America
ISBN: [ISBN number with hyphens]
Library of Congress Control Number: has been applied for.
Cover design: Jan Berger

Cover Photo: Taken by U.S. Navy photo by Mass Communication
Specialist 1st Class James E. Foehl. This file is a work of a sailor or
employee of the U.S. Navy, taken or made as part of that person's official
duties. As a work of the U.S. federal government, the image is in the
public domain. This file has been identified as being free of known
restrictions under copyright law, including all related and neighboring
rights.

Printed in the United States of America.

Ursula's Yahrtzeit Candle

Steven R. Berger

This book is dedicated to the memory of my mother
Ursula Berger Felsot
and the men in her life:
Isaac Nathans, Joseph Berger, Bernie Felsot and Art Orlando.

It is also dedicated to all of Ursula's other children:
Peter Berger, Julie Felsot Schlesinger,
her grandchildren:
Sheri and Kenneth Berger, Benjamin and Emma Schlesinger;
and her great grandchildren:
Ayden Samii, and Kate and Mariah Berger;
all of whom might not be alive today
if Adolf Hitler and his fascist regime
had not been stopped in 1945.

Chapter 1

Fourscore and seven years. That may have been fine for a young country, but too long for most people. Especially herself, Ursula thought, as she moved hangers from right to left in a small closet. In her lifetime she had gone from an abundance of clothes in a large home, to just what could be crammed into a suitcase at four in the morning. Then only to the rags on her back. Providence smiled on her as her family struggled to make a new life in a strange country, and then good fortune rewarded them when they were finally able to immigrate to the United States. That led to a steady increase in her stepfather's prosperity. So their small house with its small closets was traded up to near the elegance and style the family enjoyed before. She married well. Had children. Closets got larger again, filled with nice clothes, many shoes, but not an overabundance of anything. She had learned that more is not always better. And now, at 87, it was a smaller closet to fit her diminutive needs. Some long skirts, blouses, a few dresses she never wore, a dozen pairs of pants, even a pair of jeans she was coaxed into buying by her daughter and granddaughter, but would not be seen dead in. Once fashionable shoes had given way to sensible flats, loafers and tennis shoes, which she had to admit, were her favorite.

* * *

Reuben Montanez was considering wearing the Dodgers jersey with his name on the back. It wasn't actually his name. It was the last name of one of the team's lesser known players from several years earlier, but it was the same as his. His brother had gotten it for Christmas a few years ago. When Reuben's brother died, the jersey, and Julian's other meager possessions, fell to Reuben. But the jersey was what he loved best. His friends would laugh if they knew that he washed the shirt himself by hand—in cold water—with Woolite—so it would, he hoped, last yet another year. He decided not to wear it tonight. He feared it might get torn, or soiled beyond his ability to clean it. And he just couldn't afford that, financially or emotionally.

* * *

Ursula decided on a matching top and bottom of "active separates," as the department stores called them. Her grandson called them "lady sweats," the kind Betty White wears in that sitcom. Pastel pink, white piping, comfortable over the Depends she would wear, just in case. The outfit went well with the white tennis shoes. An expensive-looking white knockoff purse and a string of pearls would make it look like she had money, if not on her person, then in some nearby ATM.

Ursula Frank took off her trifocals to pull on a light knit top with long sleeves. She replaced her glasses and tucked the top into her pink fleece pants when the phone rang. Must be 7:45, she thought as she answered. It was her daughter, Deborah. She called every night at 7:45. She said it was because she wanted to make sure she didn't interrupt her mother's dinner or her bedtime. Although Ursula appreciated Deborah's concern, she knew the timing was based on Deborah and Sam wanting to watch whatever was on TV in primetime, so she made sure to keep her conversations to ten or twelve minutes.

This evening they talked about what everyone had for dinner, how the kids were doing now that school was back in session—her granddaughter was a senior in high school, her grandson a sophomore in college. If Deborah had just had one-third more kid and a dog, Ursula thought, she and Sam would have the perfect American family.

Ursula's son, Mike, or Moishe as it said on his birth certificate, only called once a week. His calls came on Sunday. The times varied by basketball and baseball season, and also by whether the Dodgers and the Lakers were playing at home or away. The schedule hadn't changed from her days in Sun City. Mike was divorced and, so far, had only produced a grandson, Justin, who was still in junior high and had dubbed Ursula's fleece outfits "lady sweats," a double entendre, he had proudly announced.

As this was Thursday, she could count on at least two days—and more likely, three—before Mike would call her. And nearly twenty-four hours before Deborah would check in.

* * *

Instead of the jersey, Reuben picked out a yellow and black checked shirt that was a size too big for him. The oversized shirt was part of the uniform, buttoned to the neck, short sleeves, hanging outside the baggy jeans his mother would never let him wear, if she were there to object. But his mother was working, as usual. It was nighttime, so she was behind the counter at the liquor store a few blocks away. If it was daytime, then she would be at the

2

dry cleaning plant, inhaling toxic fumes as she purged soil, food, wine, sweat and other stains from the expensive fabrics of rich white folks.

Reuben barely remembered his father. He left when Reuben was about four. His brother Julian was eight then. He told Reuben exciting stories about their father when their mother was at work, which seemed like all the time. How smart he was, how brave he had been in Vietnam, how he was going to come back someday and buy a house for the boys and their mom, and everyone would be happy.

* * *

Ursula answered the phone cheerfully. She didn't want Deborah to think there was anything different about tonight. If Deborah had been listening closely, it might have dawned on her that Ursula was more upbeat than usual, but her attention was on the clock, instead of the conversation, caused her to overlook this subtle anomaly.

In truth, Ursula's mood had been declining gradually, but steadily, since about a month after arriving in the L.A. area. She had been cajoled into moving to the Southern California megalopolis by both her children, though Deborah was more of a driving force than Mike. After raising their children in California, Ursula and her second husband, Bernie, retired from the business they built together and moved to Sun City, Arizona. They lived there for nearly twenty years before Bernie reached for a bowl of artificial sweetener at breakfast and fell dead across the table, spilling his unsweetened decaf onto the vinyl floor of their two-bedroom bungalow.

It shouldn't have been a surprise, given what the doctors had been telling him, but one is always startled when it happens. Ursula had seen death before, but never so quick and peaceful. Bernie just laid there on the table, his head turned toward the wife he adored, his gray-blue eyes sparkling with love as his soul said goodbye.

* * *

It wasn't until Reuben was twelve that he accepted the fact that his father was never going to be coming back. There would be no nice house. The family would never be together. He wanted to be angry with his brother Julian for lying to him. But Julian had sacrificed so much. He worked all the way through high school to help their mother. His teachers said he showed promise and should go to college. But there wasn't money or time for college. Julian could only get menial jobs, telling Reuben how this one or that one would grow into something big. But if something went wrong, or business was slow, it was always Julian who got blamed or laid off. From working the docks at the Central Market in downtown L.A. to hawking sodas at Dodger Stadium, Julian kept telling himself and his family that this was the job that would lead to a promotion, more money and a better life for them all.

* * *

Ursula envied Bernie now. She also envied Josef, her first husband, Art, her last boyfriend and Marty, a favored companion. All dead. Each seemed to have just suddenly left the room; Josef and Art went off to hospitals under their own steam, then laid down and died within a few days. Marty just went to sleep one night and never woke up. Even many of the women in her life, friends and relatives alike were able to escape their bodies and minds and set their souls free. But her body, painful and degenerating as it was, wouldn't quit. Neither would her mind. And, she now felt that she had a very real lapse in judgment when she finally acquiesced to her children's wishes and moved from Sun City to L.A.

"Mom, you'll be so much more comfortable here. The weather is more mild, we can visit you more often, take you places. You will be able to enjoy your grandchildren and watch them grow," Deborah pleaded and Mike quietly agreed.

"But dear," Ursula said, "I have friends here I've known for years. We play cards. Someone always has a car so we can shop, go to movies, have lunch. Really, I'm fine. Besides, you're busy working and raising your family, so is Mike. And the kids, they want to 'do their own thing,' as they say." Unfortunately, Deborah finally won out. But worse, Ursula was right.

* * *

Unfortunately, Julian Montanez was wrong about his dream of a better life for his family.

One sunny afternoon in the fifth inning of a game against the San Francisco Giants, Fernando Montanez was called up from the bench to replace the starting shortstop. In the next inning Montanez picked up a ground ball, threw it to first for an out. The first baseman then threw it back to Montanez who ran down the

4

Giants' runner trying to make his way back to second base. It was a spectacular double play by Montanez. Julian was all smiles, bouncing so much he lost his footing and would have fallen down the steps if he hadn't put his hand on the shoulder of the man seated on the aisle. The man flinched and pushed Julian's arm yelling, "Get your filthy Mexican hands off me." Trying to regain his balance, Julian shifted his weight to his left leg before rocking back onto his right. By this time the man had gotten up and Julian's tray of sodas hit him in the hip. The man pulled back his right arm and threw a fist at Julian. Julian pulled his torso to the right and the man's fist went flying past Julian's head. The force of the attempted blow caused the man to fall forward into Julian, and both men went tumbling down the steps toward the Dodgers' dugout.

Even though no punches landed, both men looked like they had gone a round with Mike Tyson. Gashes and bruises abounded. Blood dripped from noses, lips and eye sockets.

When stadium security arrived, the man was shouting that Julian had attacked him for no reason. Julian tried to explain to security what had happened. Stadium security took each man to a separate room for questioning. They then turned Julian over to the L.A.P.D. who put him in a holding cell pending an arraignment. Julian asked to call his mother. An officer pointed to a pay phone on the wall. Julian removed a wad of singles and fives totaling $38 dollars that was still in his trousers from selling sodas, then reached down to retrieve some coins. A large man with many tattoos saw the bills, took two strides across the cell, wrapped one massive arm around Julian's neck, jerked back, and removed the bills from his hand as Julian's lifeless body slumped toward the floor.

No one in the holding cell saw anything.

Chapter 2

Ursula took the elevator from the second floor of the two-story assisted-living facility to the lobby. "My son's going to pick me up outside," she told the Filipino woman at the front desk. "I'll just wait for him by the palm tree."

"You have a nice visit with your family, Ursula," she said in a voice that belonged in a choir.

Ursula pressed the automatic opener pad for the glass double doors of the facility and passed through into the mild evening twilight. She placed one hand on the brick wall of a tall planter next to the entry, walked slowly along the planter and then moved to a handrail to help her go down the five steps to street level. She could have taken the wheelchair ramp, but it would take longer, and she was still able to manage steps, up or down, as long as there weren't too many. She reached the palm tree that was just out of sight of the front desk at almost the same time as the cab she had called for earlier.

"Where to, ma'am?" the cabby asked.

Ursula handed him an address.

"Are you sure, ma'am? That's a pretty rough part of town."

"Oh yes, I know, but I'll be fine. It's a friend's place and I've been there a hundred times," she lied in her soft German accent.

"Okay, you're the boss" he said, making an on-the-spot decision to keep this one off the books. His home wasn't too much farther than the address she had given him. It was close to his normal quitting time, so if he called in and said he was done for the day, no one would suspect one last fare. He called in and told his dispatcher that the fare in the Valley was a no-show and that he was calling it a night. Then, without starting the meter, he pulled the brightly-colored taxi away from the curb.

As they drove through the thinning traffic toward downtown Los Angeles' east side, the driver talked about the weather, sports, the smog, the subway, the tourists. A running commentary on life in L.A. designed to ingratiate his fare and increase his tip. Ursula reflexively 'ummed' and affirmed where appropriate without really listening.

Her mind was on the task at hand. The address she had written down was a house number she found on Google, a discipline she was taught by one of her grandsons. They had shown her how to find their home, to look down on it as if from a cloud. And, she used it to show them some of the places she had lived; she remembered the addresses or location of each; first Berlin, then Königsberg in Poland, and then the Free City of Danzig that was neither Poland nor Germany—and now known as Gdansk. Her last stop in Europe was Amsterdam, then on to Havana, New York, Los Angeles, Sun City and finally Encino. It was hard to tell whether they were more impressed with her computer skills or her world travels.

The address she gave the cabby was in the same neighborhood where the papers reported a lot of gang activity; gangs fighting over turf, members getting beaten up and shot, businesses being vandalized, even a body being found.

It was a desperate plan, but she wanted out, and this seemed like as good a way as any. She had heard of suicide by policeman, where some schmuck hurts or even kills innocent bystanders so the police will just shoot him dead. But she didn't want to hurt anyone to accomplish her goals. She was already dying inside. Her body having more and more pain, her freedoms diminishing, and the fear that her mind would go before she did. She should have never left Sun City to come to this lonely place, she thought. The promises of more family lasted about two weeks. They gave way to, "We'll do that soon, we've got lots of time to spend together now."

Her plan was simple, at least to her. Get dropped off in this battle zone, walk around a bit looking like easy money, then get mugged. Maybe some gang ruffian would try to grab her purse. She would resist. Then maybe another gang member would hit her over the head. That's all it should take, she thought. Someone comes up from behind her with a pipe or a stick and cracks her head open like a soft-boiled egg.

Then the gang members would melt into the night, never to be seen or punished. Or, so what if they got caught. They're just a bunch of hooligans. They would deserve whatever punishment they got; for they certainly would be guilty of killing her, and undoubtedly, if you could believe the media, hundreds of other crimes.

Chapter 3

It had been a few years since Julian had been killed in an L.A.P.D. holding cell. No one was ever charged with the crime, much less convicted. As far as anyone could tell, the white guy the police said Julian attacked was released at Dodger Stadium. Nobody knew his name or even had a description. Nobody ever found out what really happened. Reuben and his mother didn't believe the police report. Reuben and his mother didn't believe the priest who told them that sometimes even good boys like Julian make a mistake. Reuben didn't believe the TV or the news or the priest, or even the words of his late brother, when they told him that joining a gang wasn't the way out.

At seventeen Reuben was approached by his friend Marco. Marco had some really cool high-tops, a really cool jacket, a really cool smartphone, and a really hot girlfriend. Marco was in a gang. The gang made some money by stealing cars, stripping them down and selling the parts, or working them over so they could be sold. But most of their money came from selling crack and Oxycontin-like pills. Sometimes they even moved a little heroin. The gang members weren't allowed to use the crack, pills or smack. They could drink, smoke cigarettes, use marijuana, and try LSD, but the gang leaders wouldn't let them get strung out on the hard stuff. Then they just became a liability; getting fucked up and being a fuck-up.

Reuben was cool with that. He would just be supplying what folks wanted. If they didn't get their high from the gang, they would get it somewhere else. The money he could make would buy him some nice threads and things. Girls would notice. And, maybe his mama wouldn't have to work two jobs. Yeah, he'd help out like Julian tried to, only better.

Reuben had been hanging with the gang for three or four months. They seemed to like him. They wanted him in the gang. He did what he was told. People liked him. He could sell shit.

This night was going to be special. This night he would be getting his colors. A simple black and red bandana to show that he is a member of the *Diecinueves*, the Nineteenth Street Gang. A new family for Reuben. These days there wasn't a single member who lived on Nineteenth Street. It wasn't even part of their turf any more, but the *Diecinueves* had a long history: Their name was adopted in the 1940s, but the roots of the gang went back more than 100 years.

"You ready for tonight, bitch?" Marco asked, as Reuben opened the front door of the apartment where he lived with his mother. She worked so much she had never even seen Marco, much less the ink lines that crept up the back of his neck from under his collar. They were the radiating light behind the virgin of Guadalupe tattoo that covered nearly his entire back. There were other tattoos on both his arms, but nothing as spectacular as the virgin; the only one in his life, he liked to joke.

Reuben was already thinking about what tattoos he wanted. For the time being, they were just in his head. He wanted to sport some ink like all the other members of the *Diecinueves*, but he didn't want his mother to see them, to ask him about them. That meant putting them off for awhile, maybe even until he turned eighteen, or moved out of her home.

"*Sí, esé*," he told his friend, in a seldom used, arcane expression.

"If you get caught, you know you're going to get roughed up," Marco said.

"I can handle it, man."

"Cops don't like spics anyway. They catch you trying to steal a car, they're going to beat the shit outta you."

"I told you, man, I can handle it, I ain't no pussy."

"You better be ready, 'cause you rat out any *Diecinueves*, what the cops do to you ain't nothin' compared to what we'll do to you."

It was the first time since he had met him that Reuben heard Marco draw a distinction between the gang and himself. It was a subtle differentiation in syntax, but Reuben was sharp enough to hear it, loud and clear. If something goes wrong tonight, he was on his own, just like when Julian died.

"I told you, bitch, I can handle it."

"Okay, bro," Marco was suddenly conciliatory. "Here, take this," he continued, handing Reuben a black and red bandana, "but keep it in your pocket until we're done, until you've earned it. Now, let's get you into *la familia*."

* * *

Reuben met Marco in his auto-shop class about six months earlier. They were rebuilding the fuel injection system of an eight-year-old Honda one of the teachers had lent the class to work on.

9

Marco noticed that Reuben was quickly picking up on how the intricate engine parts worked. He knew the *Diecinueves* could use this kind of talent. Over the next few months he found out about Reuben's mom and his brother Julian. He told Reuben that he understood how he felt, that his mother didn't have time for him, she probably had loved Julian more because he was older and helped out more; that Julian had been fucked over by the system, the white people's system that took the word of whites, blacks, Asians and Jews over Hispanics every time.

Marco also started to teach Reuben things that weren't on the auto shop curriculum, like how to slide a flat piece of metal called a jimmy between a car's window and the weather seal, hook it around the unseen mechanism in the door and pop open the lock.

Marco's hands-on lessons stopped abruptly after a couple of months when he dropped out of school. He was flunking every class except gym and auto shop. In other words, any class that required reading. Perhaps it was dyslexia. More likely it was the time he spent with the *Diecinueves* instead of studying.

That left Reuben on his own to figure out how to punch out the receptacle on a steering column, without damaging the housing, and pulling out the entire mechanism to hot wire the ignition. That was what was required of him to become a full-fledged member of the gang. He needed to steal the car the gang had chosen, then drive it to the garage they used to strip it, chop it and part it out.

Was he ready for tonight? He certainly thought so, though, of course, he had never actually hot-wired a car, it wasn't something one could do on a Honda in the high school auto shop.

Chapter 4

Ursula's taxi pulled up in front of the address she had given the cabby forty-five minutes earlier. "That's $34.75," the cabby turned to tell her. She pulled two $20 bills from her purse and told him to keep the change, exactly what he hoped she'd say. He pocketed the money and opened his door so he could get out to help her, but she stopped him and, saying she could manage, pulled her small frame up out of the back seat, leaned for a moment on the open door, and then walked slowly with forced stability toward the building, grabbing hold of a stair rail to pull herself up the entry steps.

About halfway up, she turned and gave a wave to the cabby to let him know she was doing fine. He pulled away from the curb, satisfied he had done everything that was expected of him.

When the cab had turned the corner, Ursula came back down the entry steps to the sidewalk and turned to shuffle on up the street. She felt no fear or regret.

She rounded the next corner and saw half a dozen male Mexicans ranging in age from sixteen to their early twenties taking up the entire sidewalk. Nearly half them were smoking cigarettes. She braced herself and walked toward them. As she came up to the small group, they separated like the Red Sea to let her through. When she passed, one of the kids took a long drag on his smoke. Exhaling he warned, "*Abuela, cuidado, este es un mal barrio!*" Then another translated for her, "He says this is a bad neighborhood, grandmother. Be careful."

She understood what the gang member said without the need for translation, but didn't understand why he was warning her. She thought she was going to get mugged. Why didn't they do anything to her? Why did they just stand aside and tell her to be careful? Twice even. Once in Spanish and once in English. *Abuela*, they called her. She had always liked that. It was much more lyrical than the German *Oma* she was raised with, and even the English Grandma that was now her moniker, when the family made time to visit.

Confused, she turned the next corner where there were two more Mexican boys. One was leaning up against a building. He was smoking a cigarette and trying to look casual as he glanced furtively up and down the street. The other was doing something to a nice-looking blue Toyota; leaning into the car, he was working a piece of metal up and down against the window in an almost obscene manner. Down the jimmy went, then it came back up slowly, then a pause, a jerk, and the kid would swear in disappointment and down the jimmy would go again.

Ursula had seen this on television. They were trying to break into the car. She remembered the anguish of her daughter Deborah when her car had been stolen. Without thinking she made toward the car thief. But before she got there he jerked the jimmy up one more time and heard the rewarding sound of the lock clicking open. At nearly the same instant, the boy on lookout flicked his lit cigarette aside and pushed himself away from the building to intercept Ursula.

Down they both tumbled, she, cushioning his fall and banging her scalp against the concrete sidewalk. Blood start to ooze through her white hair, her arm twisted at an odd angle beneath her.

Marco jumped up off his prey. Startled, panicked and off balance, he fell backwards against the Toyota, steadied himself against the rear door with both hands, then twisted his body 180 degrees and pushed off against the car, regaining his balance. "Shit, man, we gotta get outta here," he yelled at Reuben. The younger boy was flustered. What just happened? He had unlocked the car door. An old woman was trying to come toward him. Marco jumped on her. She's lying on the ground, bleeding. Dead? Marco had fallen on the woman, got up, gained his footing, and was now running toward the corner where the other members of the *Diecinueves* were waiting. What the fuck?

Despite his confusion, Reuben kneeled down next to Ursula. She was breathing hard, moaning and trying to free the arm pinned under her while reaching up to her head with her free hand. Reuben looked up the street to find Marco, to tell him to go get help, but the street was empty. Two or three cars passed by, but the drivers couldn't see Reuben and Ursula on the sidewalk; parked cars hid them from view.

"Please try to stay calm," Reuben inexplicably told Ursula. "I'm going to try to help you. Just stay here, *un momentito, por favor.*"

She stared up at him. She must be going into shock, she thought, as she relaxed her body despite the pain it placed on her pinned arm.

Reuben suddenly remembered the bandana Marco had given him. He took the sacred symbol of *Diecinueves* membership from his pocket and pressed it into place between Ursula's good hand and her skull. He got up and wheeled back to the blue Toyota, picking up the jimmy and other tools in a graceful scoop. He opened the unlocked passenger door and lay down in a prone position on the seat as he jammed a large screwdriver into the keyhole on the steering column. He held the assembly in place as he tighten the grip on a pair of channel locks around the ignition's housing. The pliers-looking device slipped, so he repositioned his tools and tried again. Slip, scratch. Again; slip, scratch. Two more times until there was finally enough "tooth" for the channel locks to grip.

The muscles in his thin arms stretched, the tendons becoming visible beneath his coffee-brown skin. Finally, the mechanism came forth in agonizing micro-millimeters. When its housing was clear of the steering column, Reuben quickly stripped the insulation from four of the wires. He twisted two together and then touched the other two to make the engine come to life.

He backed out of the car on his elbows and went over to Ursula. She wasn't moving. The hand that held the *Diecinueves* bandana to her head had gone limp. She had stopped bleeding. She was either unconscious or dead.

Reuben put his hand to her neck like he'd seen on TV, but he had no idea what she was supposed to feel like. But she didn't feel too cold, so maybe she was going to be okay. He wasn't sure what to do. Everything was going so fast, and now it was slowing down, down, down.

He fought the urge to run after Marco, to take refuge in the safety of the *Diecinueves*.

Then he thought of his mother and his brother Julian. Suddenly it wasn't an old white woman lying on the sidewalk, it was his mother, Maria. Suddenly there wasn't a gang just around the corner—if indeed they were still there—it was his brother, waiting to see what Reuben would do, waiting for him to bring their mother to him.

Reuben had no first-aid training. He didn't know that if you suspected a fracture or shock, you're not supposed to move the body. All he knew was that somebody's mother was lying on the sidewalk in front of him. She had been bleeding from a head

13

wound; and that couldn't be good. The bleeding had stopped; he hoped that was a good sign, and not a sign that she had died.

He slid his arms under the frail body and lifted, straining his young back. As the weight was removed from Ursula's pinned arm, she let out an involuntary groan. She was still alive. She was easy to carry once Reuben straightened up. He took four steps over to the blue Toyota and folded her into the passenger seat, even taking a moment to buckle her seatbelt—the last thing he wanted was for a cop to pull him over in a stolen car because his passenger wasn't wearing her seatbelt.

He clicked the unlock button on the passenger door and went around to the driver's side, opened the door, slid in, buckled his seatbelt and pulled away from the curb. He started to drive toward L.A. Central Memorial Hospital, but then his mind reeled ahead to his image of the waiting room, the officious staff, the paperwork, the questions. He veered into the left lane, then the turn lane, and then onto a smaller street that would take him to the Chavez Clinic.

The clinic was located in a store that used to be a pharmacy between a dollar store and a used appliance shop. His mother had brought him here a couple of times to patch up school yard scrapes and one time with a fractured forearm. They were staffed by either a doctor or nurse practitioner from L.A. Central Memorial for the serious cases. The scrapes, minor burns, light cuts, shallow punctures were often treated by nursing or medical school students, aspiring young volunteers and people doing community service, as prescribed by the courts.

By and large, the volunteer staff were long on compassion and short on paperwork; the most important being a waiver so they didn't get sued, which would shut down the clinic.

Reuben pulled the blue Toyota up to the passenger loading area in front of the clinic, then, realizing the police might come looking for the stolen car at any time, he pulled away from the curb to look for a parking space up the block. Before the car had even come to a complete stop, Reuben grabbed at the wires hanging off the steering column and yanked them apart, then danced swiftly around the car to the other side.

He opened the passenger door and picked up Ursula again. She gave a soft groan and opened her eyes. She looked confused rather than frightened, Reuben thought, hoping he was right. The arm that had been twisted under her fell limp across her stomach,

14

the other swung loosely from the side away from Reuben. As Reuben backed the two of them through the door of the clinic, a Hispanic girl about Reuben's age looked up from an old counter that had been donated to the clinic from an out-of-business shoe store in the neighborhood.

"What's wrong with her?" the girl asked.

"She fell down some steps and hurt her head," Reuben repeated the story he had been rehearsing in his head.

"Is she a relative?" the girl asked.

He hadn't anticipate that question, "Ah, yeah, she's ah, my grandmother."

The girl looked skeptical. Ursula caught Reuben's eye. He thought he saw the look his mother would give him when she had a surprise for him. He looked at the girl again and noticed she was wearing a badge with her name, Olivia Carillo. "Your grandmother?" she asked.

After what seemed like an eternity, Ursula looked toward Olivia and said, "*Sí, es verdad. Yo soy de España, de San Sebastian.*"

Chapter 5

Olivia was so startled by Ursula's flawless, though accented, Spanish, she didn't notice Reuben suddenly jerk up an inch, opening his eyes so wide his brows wrinkled up onto his forehead.

Olivia regained her composure and asked Reuben, "What's your grandmother's name."

"*Me llama es Ursula*," Reuben's charge answered before he could blurt out a moniker neither of them would remember.

"Ursula what?" Olivia asked.

"Montanez," Reuben answered with a smile, "Ursula Montanez. Originally from San Sebastian, Spain." He liked the idea of having a Spanish grandmother, instead of the Mexican grandparents he had never known. "And Ursula Montanez needs to have a doctor look at her right away," he finished with pride.

Having Reuben take over the situation allowed Ursula to relax a little. She also liked his apparent adoption of her so much that she forgot why she had wanted to come down to this part of the city, and the role that Reuben had played in putting her into her current situation; possible fracture, possible concussion, definite lacerations that needed attention, maybe even stitches. All of that was beside the point for her now.

"Can you stand on your own now, *abuela*?" Reuben asked Ursula.

"*Sí, sí, gracias me hijo*," she replied, coherent enough to stay in character.

"About the doctor?" Reuben turned his attention back to Olivia.

"Certainly ah, . . . Mr. Montanez? Of course, we need to have someone look at your, ah, grandmother, but, there's no doctor and Nurse Practitioner Soto is busy with a stab . . . I mean, puncture wound. Carlos can see her in a few minutes. Please take a seat and fill out this form."

"Can't *you* do something, ah, Olivia," he took his eyes off hers long enough to read the name badge on her left breast. Aren't you a nurse?"

"No. It's a little confusing 'cause we all wear scrubs here. I'm kind of a, umm, volunteer. Here, fill this out and someone will see your grandma in a few minutes."

"Please, she was bleeding a lot from her head."

16

"I know you're worried about her, but head wounds always bleed a lot. Your *abuela* is actually doing pretty good. She understands you in both Spanish and English. She's going to be alright. It'll just be a few minutes, honest."

Reuben helped Ursula gently over to the waiting area where they sat down in folding chairs with padded, faux-leather seats, split from age. Reuben started to fill in the form but didn't get far; the clinic wanted an address for its patient. He didn't have an address for Ursula. He couldn't put in his own address. He thought about the garage where the *Diecinueves* brought cars to be dismantled or altered so their parts could be sold, or sold as-is with a VIN plaque they got from a junk yard, usually in a different state. He was stumped. He just couldn't think of an address that sounded legitimate. He looked up at Olivia and suddenly a thought popped into his head and he filled in the address and phone number boxes with confidence.

There was also a line on the form asking who would take financial responsibility for the patient. Some lawyer's idea of a joke, Reuben thought. Who the hell had money for hospitals and doctors in this part of L.A.? What a schmuck, whoever decided to include that line. He put down "J. Montanez," thinking of his deceased brother. Try to collect from him, assholes.

"Mr. Montanez, Carlos can see your grandmother now. Let me help you take her into the exam room." Olivia got on one side of Ursula, gently holding onto her elbow but ready to reach out in case she started to fall. Reuben had his arm around Ursula's waist as the trio walked slowly down a short hallway with "rooms" that had curtains for walls. This area was obviously where the clinic put what little money it had. The wall at the back was painted a semi-gloss off-white. The examination tables showed wear but were clean and sanitary. Spotless instrument trays rested on stands that had their wear camouflaged under glossy black paint. All very clean and serviceable.

Olivia guided Ursula and Reuben into one of the cubicles. All three turned completely around so the two young people could back Ursula gently onto the exam table. "You can wait with her until Carlos comes in," she said. "He'll want to examine her in private, so just bring me your paperwork then."

"Is Carlos a doctor or nurse or something?" Reuben asked.

"He's almost a doctor."

"Almost a doctor, what the hell does that mean?"

17

"It's okay. He has one more year of medical school before he starts his residency. But he's been working here for two years. He's very good, honest. He's under the supervision of Dr. Dreyfus . . . "

"But you said the doctor wasn't here?"

"No, not now, but he's supervised Carlos for two years. It'll be okay. If it's more serious than Carlos can handle, we'll call an ambulance to take your *abuela* to L.A. Central, trust me."

Reuben was stymied, what would happen if Ursula went to the big hospital? There would be questions. They might call the cops. They would want to talk to him. He couldn't let that happen, but he also couldn't let Ursula go without seeing a doctor, or an almost-doctor.

Trying to hide his anxiety he asked, "You'll tell me if you need to call an ambulance, won't you? I mean, I want to come along or meet her there, you know? I don't want her to be there alone." He hoped his words showed concern for Ursula, but his rapid-fire speech was coming across as nervous and frightened. What he really wanted was for Olivia to let him know if they called an ambulance so he could get a head start. He figured he could be out the door and back with the gang in ten minutes, if they were still out and about; it was getting late.

Sensing his anxiety, Olivia did her best to reassure him, while wondering what was really wrong, and if she should call the police. She didn't want to call the cops. She had only had to do that once with an out-of-control junkie. Then they just swooped in, tazed the miscreant, asked for her name, and left. That was often how things got done in the *barrio*. They never followed up with her or anyone else at the clinic. For all she knew, they had dumped the poor paralyzed bastard into the dry concrete culvert formerly known as the Los Angeles River.

Bringing her thoughts back to Ursula and Reuben she said, "Look, everything's going to be okay. Your grandma's doing fine. Look at her, man. She's following everything we're saying; she's not staring off into space or passed out. She'll be okay. Don't worry about her, don't worry about the hospital, okay?"

Reuben looked at Ursula who had been following their conversation but saying nothing. Her head had stopped bleeding some time ago, the blood caked against her thin white hair and pale, nearly translucent, skin. But her eyes were clear and seemed to dance as her gaze went from Reuben to Olivia, then back again.

"Do you think she's right, *abuela*?" Reuben asked Ursula.

She nodded ever so slightly with a hint of smile. "I'll be fine, *hijo*," she said, remembering to stay in character by flavoring her answer with a pinch of Spanish as a short Hispanic man in hospital-teal scrubs came in.

"Hello, I'm Carlos Bienventura," he said to Reuben and Ursula before turning his attention to Olivia, "who have we here?"

"This is Ursula Montanez and her grandson, ah . . . "

"Reuben," Reuben said.

"Yes," Olivia continued. "Reuben, Reuben Montanez. He brought his grandmother in. He said she fell. There was lots of blood from her head, and her left arm got twisted under her."

"Thank you Olivia. Would you show Mr. Montanez out while I examine his grandmother."

During the course of his examination, Carlos Bienventura casually asked Ursula again what had happened, since too many cases like hers are the result of neglect and even violence from a family member or caregiver. Too often the proverbial fall is really the outcome of an argument over money or living conditions that flares up into a physical fight or the beating of an older family member by a child or grandchild.

Ursula stuck to the story Reuben started. No embellishments, no tales or convoluted details she would have to remember. Just a simple fall down a few steps. Bienventura couldn't tell if she was telling the truth about the fall or not, but the rest of his examination at least, confirmed that Ursula had not been the victim of a fight or beating—the major reason for examining her without her grandson in the room.

* * *

Olivia took the form from Reuben as they walked the short distance back to the waiting room.   She looked over the papers as they walked, noting that Reuben's answer to Ursula's age was 90. If he wasn't right on, then he hadn't guessed too far from the truth, she thought. She kept reading as they entered the waiting room. Reuben took his former seat and she resumed her position at the second-hand counter. Then she looked up at him, stared for a moment and then headed back to the examination area.

When she was in front of the cubicle with Ursula, she asked Carlos Bienventura if she could come in for just a moment.

"Is it just you?" he said.

19

"Yes. Reu . . . , the grandson said there was something of his he needed. Can I come in for a second?"

"Yes, but be quick."

With practiced skill, she moved the curtain just enough to slip through. She looked around the room and then saw what she thought she had remembered. There, on the edge of the bed, wadded up and barely identifiable was the *Diecinueves* bandana; black and red, and stained with Ursula's blood.

Chapter 6

"Is this what you used to stop the bleeding?" Olivia clenched the blood-stained bandana before Reuben's face, her rage made her hand tremble as though stricken with Parkinson's disease. It was late and, except for a mother with a sick child, there was no one else in the front of the clinic.

"I, uh, yeah, umm, it was near where she fell. Just some rag. What about it?"

"You know damn well what about it," she straddled the chair in front of him and sat down, her face just inches from his.

"It's just a shitty piece of old rag, bitch. Get outta my face, huh."

"It's not just some shitty piece of old rag, asshole, and you know it," a droplet of spit inadvertently launched from her mouth. "Just like you know that address and phone number don't belong to your *abuela*. *Abuela*, my ass. That's the address and phone number of your high school . . ."

"Hey girl . . ."

"Don't you 'Hey girl' me, *pachuco*. You're just another one of those *Diecinueves* thugs." At the mention of the gang, the woman with the sick child snatched up her son and disappeared through the front door.

"What happened?" Olivia continued without even noticing the woman leaving the clinic, "You try to steal her purse and she screamed or something? Then you beat her up? Beating up a poor little old lady, tough guy, huh. Is that what happened?"

"No girl, you got it all wrong. She's my grandma, she speaks Spanish. Where you gonna to find an old white lady that speaks Spanish?"

"That don't mean shit. You told her what to say didn't you?" it was a rhetorical question. "You knew you'd be in deep shit if she fingered you for trying to rob her. You probably threatened to hurt her even more if she talked."

"That's not what happened, honest." Reuben was in retreat. He looked around for an escape route, but he would have to go through Olivia to reach the door and, as panicked as he was, he didn't want to hurt anyone. "Really lady, she must know Spanish, I didn't tell her nothin'."

"She must know Spanish. Is that what you just said? You mean you didn't know she speaks Spanish?"

"Well, uh . . ."

"Bullshit. You lying fucker. She's no more your grandmother than I am. Fuck you, you woman-beating piece of shit. I'm going to call the cops, they'd love to bust a *Diecinueves* punk like you."

As Olivia rose from the chair Reuben grabbed her by the arm. "Please. Please don't call the cops. Honest, I didn't hurt her. If you call the cops it would just kill my mother. She just couldn't take losing another son."

All of Reuben's entreaties fell on deaf ears until he said that his mother "just couldn't take losing *another* son." She whipped her head around and stared down at Reuben, tears welling up in his eyes, his grip loosening on her arm. She looked from him to the form he had filled out. She saw the line for financial responsibility where "J. Montanez" was scrawled in. "You're Julian Montanez' brother, aren't you?"

"You know *mi hermano*?"

"Yeah, I knew him," Olivia said, sinking back down on the chair, but sitting sideways instead of straddling the backrest. She stared at Reuben as though she were examining the brush strokes of a fine painting. There they were, she thought. There were Julian's soft, dark eyes.

"How did you know Julian?"

"We ended up in detention together in high school, the one you wrote down the address of on your *abuela's* entry form."

"My brother. You're mistaken. My brother would never get detention. He was always the good one. Good grades, always working some job. All *mi madre* could ever talk about was how good Julian was. You're thinking of someone else."

"No, it was him. You have his eyes, you even kinda sound like him."

"I do?" Reuben said, not without some pride.

"Yeah, kid, you do."

"Kid? How old do you think I am, mama? You so much older?"

"Hey, I didn't mean anything by it. You're probably the same age as Julian when he died, huh?"

"Yeah. So how come he was in detention? And how come you were in detention?"

"Your brother had missed taking one of his finals 'cause he was working or something. His teacher said she didn't believe him, and it wouldn't matter even if it was true. So, for him to be able to retake the test, he had to do like twelve days of detention after school."

"Figures. Even when he was bad he was good."

"Not always."

"Whatdaya mean?"

She looked at the floor for a moment, then back to Reuben, "He had the reputation of being so good, that after two or three days of detention, the teacher in charge told Julian to watch over us ruffians while he went to grade papers or something."

"So, like I said, even when he was bad he was good."

"Nope. After two days of watching the teacher's pattern, instead of staying in the classroom doing homework or just sitting around, Julian took me and the other two kids to a friend's house where we played pool and drank beer—though he only let us have one bottle each. Then we'd go back to school a half hour before detention ended and the teacher would show up right on the dot to let us all go.

"But you see, even after we were done with detention, Julian helped me get my shit together. I think he liked me, you know, as a girl, like, uh, well, anyway, I was too young for him. He was about to graduate and I was a freshman, and since I had skipped a grade in elementary school, I mean, I was really too young then."

"So, you're about my age."

"Pretty close, I guess."

"So, that was it, you guys were friends."

"More than that. We were both good students, but I kept getting into trouble. I'd cut classes, curse at teachers. End up back in detention, but not with Julian. Anyway, he thought I was too smart to keep getting detention, probably from working in the counselors' office. Then he found me and started to kinda watch out for me. Told me to come talk to him, or yell at him, even punch him if I thought it would help. He just made sure he was there if I was feeling frustrated or just pissed off. I didn't know it then, but I was one more fuck-up away from getting expelled."

"How'd you find that out? Did Julian tell you?"

"Naw. One of the counselors told me all this after he died. He convinced them that I was, in his words, 'worth saving.' He kinda cut a deal with them that if I did some community service, I could work off some of the bad shit I did. They went for it. Then he

23

convinced me that doing stuff like this would make him proud of me. That's how I ended up, uh, volunteering here."

"You like it?"

"I think I like helping people a whole bunch better than I liked hurting myself. Doing stuff here makes me feel better about myself. I'm less frustrated. I don't get into trouble anymore. So, what about you?" she asked.

"Whatdaya mean, 'what about me?'"

"Did you hurt that woman? Don't bullshit me now."

Reuben was surprised, both by the bluntness and implication of Olivia's question, and because he had forgotten all about Ursula while listening to Olivia talk about his brother and herself.

"No. No. I told you. I would never hurt an old lady. Come on, you know the *Diecinueves* and the other gangs don't mess with white folks. Shit, that would bring the cops down big time."

"Then who is she?" Olivia lowered her voice to bring him into her confidence.

In a similarly lowered voice, Reuben said, "I don't know. Really. She was just there, you know?"

"I don't know. On your brother's soul, did you hurt her?"

Stunned, Reuben looked at the floor and said, "On my brother's soul, no. I didn't hurt her."

"Okay, I'll believe you if you tell me exactly what happened. Maybe I can help."

Reuben looked into Olivia's eyes and believed he saw trust there. "I was boosting a car for the *Diecinueves*. It was part of my initiation. My friend Marco was keeping watch. I had just jimmied the lock when that old woman came walking up. She was walking right at me. I didn't know what she wanted. I didn't know what she was going to do. I was going to run, but then Marco came flying off the building like Batman or somethin' and knocked her down. Then he ran around the corner to where some other *Diecinueves* were. I think he told me to run, too. I don't remember. I was frozen. The woman was hurt. It was my fault. I couldn't just leave her. I put her into the car I was stealing and came here."

"Oh shit," Olivia said, "is the car here?"

"No. I thought about that, it's parked down the block."

"Not good enough. If the cops find it they'll be here asking questions. And you and the old lady better not be here when they come."

"Man, this sucks. I don't know where she lives. I can't take her home. Maybe I can take her to the *Diecinueves* garage with the car. That'll get rid of the car and after she's rested a little she can just go home."

"Don't you go anywhere near that car, or that gang. Didn't your brother teach you anything? The cops will be looking for that car soon enough, and the gang is just a one-way ticket to jail. "Can you take her home with you?"

"No, my mother will be getting off work at the liquor store. She'll be even more pissed at me than you are."

"Well …" Olivia started to say when Carlos Bienventura wheeled Ursula Frank "Montanez" into the waiting room.

"Your grandmother's injuries aren't as bad as they looked," he said, wheeling her over to where Reuben and Olivia were conspiring. "Her head wound was just a very bad scrape. I cleaned off all the blood and put some Aquafor on it. You should apply more for a day or two to keep the area moist and to prevent infection" he said, handing Reuben a small sample tube of the medication. "Her arm got twisted pretty bad, but nothing was broken. It's in a wrist wrap now. The sling is more to remind her not to use it than for actual need. She should ice it three or four times a day for fifteen minutes for a couple of days and take Aleve or Advil as directed on the package until she feels better. She can stop using the sling and the wrap in a few days."

"Thank you, Carlos," Olivia said, before Reuben could even open his mouth. "I'll help her grandson get her into the car."

Chapter 7

Olivia took the handles of the wheelchair and said, "Just relax Mrs. Montanez. We'll have you home in no time."

From her position, Olivia couldn't see Ursula's expression change from mildly pleasant to disappointed. It would not have mattered anyway, as all Olivia wanted to do was get Carlos out of the room so she and Reuben and Ursula could figure out what to do next.

"Thanks, Olivia," Carlos said, as he yielded the wheelchair to her care and disappeared down the hall to check on other patients.

Olivia pushed Ursula's chair toward the entry door and stopped as soon as Carlos was safely out of hearing range. She came around to the front of the chair and crouched down on her heels. "Mrs. Mont . . . , ah, hey, I know you're not Reuben's *abuela*. So, what's your real name?"

Ursula looked at Olivia and just shook her head.

"Come on hon," Olivia said soothingly, as if she were trying to comfort a child. "Please tell us who you are. We want to help you. We want to get you out of this neighborhood and back to your home."

Ursula shook her head again.

"*Abuela*," Reuben said for lack of anything to call her. "I'm really sorry for hurting you, well, for causing you to get hurt. But this is no place for you. You must have a nice home to go to, and people who will take care of you, who love you."

Ursula looked up over the heads of the young people, furrowed her brow in concentration, then lowered her gaze and shook her head again.

"Shit," Olivia said, rising up from her crouch. "Well, she can't stay here. You'll have to do something with her. But don't you go near that stolen car. I can cover for you if the cops show up, but if they find you within a hundred feet of that car, they'll throw your ass in jail for grand theft auto, and then give you the chair for kidnapping this old woman."

When Ursula heard Olivia's pessimistic prognosis, she looked up from the chair and said, "My name really is Ursula. But I don't want to go back anywhere. I haven't finished what I came here to do."

"What's that, Ursula?" Olivia asked in her professional kind voice.

"Not saying. And there's nothing you can do or say that will change my mind. I'm an old woman, and if Reuben's gang wants to beat me up, or if your clinic wants to call the cops, it doesn't scare me. I've been through much worse."

Though they doubted her claim, both young people were convinced of her passion.

"Ursula, look, you can't stay here. This is a clinic. We got all kinds of people coming and going, all day and all night. I'm sorry to say it, but you'll probably be in the way, especially in another half hour when the bars close. That's when it can get really bat shit here."

The older woman looked at the younger and pressed her lips together.

"What about your place, Reuben? Can you take her there?"

"I told you, *mi madre*, will be home soon. I can't take her there. There'll be too many questions."

"So lie to her," Olivia said. "I'm sure it won't be the first time."

"Lie how? How do I explain coming home with an old lady, huh? It's not like she's some puppy that followed me home."

Both women smiled ever so slightly at the thought of a cute little puppy following Reuben down the street to his home— though each pictured that street dramatically different from the other. The women's thin smiles vanished in a heartbeat as a police squad car drove past the clinic, its ultra-bright red, blue and white LEDs sparkling like a 4th of July celebration.

It wasn't certain that the police were homing in on the stolen car, or answering some other emergency, but it brought the possibility of coming face-to-face with assertive cops home like a slap in the face.

"Shit," Olivia said as she twirled back around the second-hand counter. Reaching low she pulled up a sizable bag and rummaged through to find her spare set of keys. "Julian, I mean Reuben, here." She tossed the keys to the young man. "My apartment, 112 Olive Street, number 527. Do you have money for a cab? Shit, forget it. There isn't any time if the cops know about the car. Just get out. You'll have to manage the old lady on your own. You can take the wheelchair, it'll be faster, but you need to take it

27

into the house so I can bring it back tomorrow. Can you do all that?"

"*Sí*, yes, *gracias*," he said pushing Ursula toward the door.

"I get off at six," Olivia called after him. "And call your *madre* so she doesn't worry about you."

He waved a hand back over his head to let her know he heard her.

"And don't fuck with any of my stuff," she whispered into the night, knowing he couldn't hear her anymore, "or I'll tell your *hermano* to kick your ass," she finished even more quietly, thinking of Julian and how proud he would be of her helping his little brother.

Chapter 8

As Reuben raced the wheelchair down the ADA ramp Ursula said, "Slow down, *hijo*. If your friend didn't kill me, then you will. Besides, you can't race a wheelchair through the streets, it looks as suspicious as it is. The cops will have us both arrested."

Reuben immediately slowed down, more at the surprise of his charge speaking so forcefully and clearly, than for what she actually said.

"Now you decide to talk. You going to tell me your name and where you live, grandma?"

"I told you, my name is Ursula. You can call me that or *abuela*, I kinda like that. It reminds me of the years I spent in Cuba."

"Cuba? You gotta be kidding. How did you end up in Cuba?" he said as he turned the wheelchair up the block in the opposite direction of the stolen car.

"That's a long story. Today my address is 112 Olive Street, apartment 527," she smiled after giving him Olivia Carillo's address.

While Ursula was feeling self-satisfied for the moment, the reality of what Reuben was doing made him break out in a sweat. What was he going to tell his mother? What if there was someone else at Olivia's, like her mother? Or worse, her father or a brother that would kick his ass. Surely she wouldn't have given him the key and told him to go there if there was any possibility of that. If not for his sake, or the memory of his brother, then for the sake of their patient.

While he was mulling over those thoughts and pushing the wheelchair through the nearly deserted, early morning streets of downtown Los Angeles, LAPD officers pulled up adjacent to the stolen blue Toyota so the rear license plate was visible.

The cop riding shotgun punched the plate number into a laptop computer bolted to a stand connected to the dash. In a moment, the computer screen let him know that this car was reported stolen a few hours ago, who its rightful owner was, and when and where it was last seen by that owner. Pushing another button, the cop was treated to a grainy video of the car being driven away from the crime scene, but it was too dark and far away to make out the driver. The video was from a security camera mounted on a rip-off paycheck-cashing shop, one of the few businesses that found it cost-effective to operate in that part of town.

The cops pulled their cruiser into a red zone alongside a fire hydrant, parked and locked the vehicle and began walking the neighborhood. They couldn't really canvas it as almost everyone was asleep at this hour, even the homeless people and derelicts curled up in doorways or stretched out on sheets of cardboard in alleys. Occasionally they would find someone that was awake, but bleary-eyed and unaware of the car or anyone that may have come from it.

It didn't take long for the cops to find the clinic, about the only thing open at that hour. As Olivia predicted, several potential patients had wandered in after the bars closed. All but one was working on his paperwork, and he had already been admitted and was in an exam room with Carlos.

"Good evening ma'am," one of the cops said to Olivia. "We were wondering if you saw anything unusual in the neighborhood tonight?"

Olivia looked up from some paperwork and said without rancor or sarcasm, "Can you be a little more specific, officer? Pretty much every night is unusual around here."

"Sorry, Ms, ah, Carillo. Of course. We found a stolen car about half a block from here. We were wondering if you or anyone here happened to see anything related to it? It's a late model blue Toyota."

"Not anyone from the clinic. It's been a slow but steady night. No one from here has been outside since about eight," she answered truthfully.

"Hey," she addressed the collection of patients in the waiting area, "any of you know anything about a blue Toyota up the block? It's kinda new."

All the people in the waiting area looked around at each other, some shrugged their shoulders, none answered. "Sorry officer, wish I could be more help."

"What about people coming in tonight? Any gang members or toughs?"

"Lotsa tough people in the 'hood, ya know? But no one that's in a gang, as far as we could tell," she justified her lying by remembering that Reuben wasn't in a gang, yet—just going through the initiation to be voted in. "Just the usual moms bringing in the kids with coughs, cuts, scraps. Not even a fracture tonight—

30

well, we don't know about some of these guys yet. There was a boy, like high school age, with his grandma. She fell down some stairs. Carlos, the doc on duty, checked her out. She's going to be okay. They left like five, ten minutes ago. That's about it."

"Thanks ma'am," the cop said. He and his partner took one more look around the waiting area and left. Olivia looked back at her paperwork, closed her eyes and touched the cross that hung from her neck. Nobody noticed.

* * *

"*Hijo*, slow down. You're starting to go too fast again. One bump in the sidewalk and I'm a goner," she said to Reuben, missing the irony of her statement, since coming into downtown L.A. in the middle of the night had been her way of checking out of her mortal coil. "You're troubled. Is it because you have to lie to your mother? Or because you can't think of a credible lie to tell her?"

"Both, I guess," he huffed from the growing exertion of pushing the wheelchair up and down the gentle hills of downtown L.A.

"I doubt that it would be the first time."

Reuben didn't say anything to her, but she imagined that hidden behind her was a boy who just blushed.

"But you don't lie very often, do you?"

"No." It came out soft and low like the bottom note on a saxophone.

"Then she'll be more prone to believing you, if you don't tell her some big whopping B.S. story."

"How come you think you know so much, old lady?"

"Listen, *hijo*. I told you, you can call me Ursula or *abuela*, but show me some respect, or didn't you learn that from your *madre*?"

"Don't you say anything about *mi madre*."

"I asked if you had learned something from her, not what she tried to teach you."

Reuben didn't understand Ursula's nuanced reply, but her tone, if not the implication that she was faulting him and not his mother, kept him from pursuing it further. It was something he decided he would reexamine later, something that he wanted to understand better, like when Marcos subtly made the differentiation between Reuben and the *Diecinueves*.

31

"I'm sorry *abuela*. I'm just confused. Nothing tonight has turned out the way I planned."

"You mean because I spoiled your car theft?"

"That's only one part."

"Life is very complex, Reuben Montanez," it was the first time she had used his name. That and her reference to the car theft drove home the fact that she had been listening to everything going on around her. He suddenly grew scared. She knew his name, that he was trying to steal a car. She probably figured out the gang connection, just like Olivia Carillo had. She could simply call the police and get him into a lot of trouble. A lot of trouble because, in addition to the car theft and the gang connection, from watching police shows on television, he was fairly certain that what he was doing with her was kidnapping, or something like it, even though he didn't want to be there with her. Even though he wanted to just put her in a cab and send her home, or just leave her at the hospital.

Ursula sensed his nervousness. "It's okay, *hijo*. I don't want to get you in trouble. I'm not sure what I want. But I think I can help. Do you have a cell phone?"

"Yes, of course."

"Just stop for a moment and call your mother. If she comes home and doesn't find you there she'll be worried. She'll probably call the police and we don't want them to find us."

"How do you know what she'll do?"

"She's a mother. So am I. It's what we would do."

"What should I tell her?"

"Enough truth so your story won't come back and bite you in the butt, enough lie so she won't come looking for you, or be too angry when she finds out the whole truth."

"What makes you think she'll ever find out what's really going on?"

"Parents always do. Don't worry, it won't be the end of the world, as long you make the good outweigh the bad."

"How do I do that?"

"First, make sure you've calmed down. Moms can hear panic in their children's voices. Then tell her you were out with a friend and ran into an old friend of your brother."

Jesus, he thought, she really does listen and remember stuff.

"You got to talking and realized it was really late and, since she lived a lot closer to where you guys were, she suggested you sleep on the couch in the apartment where she lives with her mother. You'll be fine and see her in the morning."

"Apartment she shares with her mother? How do you know?"

"I don't. I just don't think she'd like you spending the night with a girl when you're still in high school. And, make sure you mention the girl's name, Olivia Carillo."

"I know here name. But what if my mother wants to talk to her mother?"

"Give the phone to me. I told you, I am a mother. I know what to say. Would it be better if I talked to her in Spanish or English?"

"Either is fine," he was still amazed that Ursula spoke Spanish, though he had never heard it spoken with her accent.

Chapter 9

Reuben made the call to his mother. The phone in their little apartment rang five times before she answered. "*Hijo*, I just came in the door, where are you?" He was glad she hadn't gotten home earlier to find him mysteriously out. He told her what Ursula said, ending with, "If you want to talk to Mrs. Carillo, I can wake her." Good touch, Ursula thought, a straight forward offer that would surely be declined, but she was ready to play her part if it came to that, it wouldn't have been the first time.

Reuben pressed End Call on his cell phone and slid the instrument back into his jeans. He began pushing the wheelchair in a smooth, even motion as if it had runners and was gliding across ice. Ursula was pleased with the calmer movement of her ride, with Reuben's good sense in not embellishing their little lie, and with herself for realizing that her instincts were still alive and well.

"Reuben, what are those lights up there?"

"Probably an all-night *bodega*."

"Let's go in and get something to eat, I'm starving," she said. Without comment he steered the wheelchair into the neighborhood convenience store. Ursula was reminded of the *bodegas* where she shopped in Havana. Tiny storefronts crammed with everything from cans of soup and *refritos* to dark, unsweetened chocolate and *ristras*—bunches of red and green chili peppers that hung from twine or were arranged in wreaths. A far cry from the sausage shops and groceries of her native Berlin, and much more colorful, vibrant and full of the promise of a bright new life. The smell of warm corn tortillas and roasted chilies evoked wonderful memories of her first taste of freedom, just like in Cuba.

Like so many hole-in-the-wall stores in the Latino part of L.A., this one was already cooking up refried beans and rolling them into tortillas along with pork, beef, chicken or chorizo scrambled eggs and potatoes, and rich yellow cheese for the rush of morning commuters and laborers. "Reuben, get us some fresh burritos, a small carton of milk for me and whatever you want to drink, a soda, milk, water, grab that too."

"*Abuela*, should you be eating that?" he knew from his relatives and the grandparents of friends, that older people didn't like spicy foods, or it wasn't so good for their digestion.

"Oh yes, my child. It's been so long. My treat."

"Okay, it's your stomach."

"The milk will take care of that."

Reuben left the wheelchair to one side of the front door so he could negotiate the aisles. He got the milk and a Pepsi from the refrigerator at the back of the store and picked up two breakfast burritos from the heated case in the front. He set them on the counter and took the bills Ursula fished out of her purse.

Once again on the sidewalk, Reuben balanced pushing the wheelchair along as he took a bite of burrito with one hand and a swig of Pepsi with the other. Ursula was as happy as a sultan in a sedan chair eating her burrito and occasionally taking a drink of milk. The couple were so involved in their beggars banquet that they didn't even notice the police squad car easing up the street until it had come even with them.

"Hey kid," the cop riding shotgun called. "You the ones that were at the clinic tonight?"

Fortunately, Reuben had a mouthful of burrito, so his probable stammered, nervous answer never erupted. Instead, Ursula swallowed hard and said, "That's us, officer. We're just having some breakfast on our way back home."

"Where's that?"

"One twelve Olive Street, apartment 527," Ursula said and smiled. Reuben had swallowed his wad of burrito but was letting his charge take point as he stared wide-eyed toward the squad car.

"You two shouldn't be out around here at this hour," that cop called back.

"We don't have a car, and we couldn't afford to have the cab that took me to the clinic wait for us. And they just don't run down here in the wee hours, you know?"

"How about we give you a lift the rest of the way?"

"Oh, it's not that much farther," Reuben finally chimed in.

"A lot can happen in a few blocks," the officer said as his partner applied the brakes and he got out. "Roll that thing over here, we'll put it in the trunk." He helped Reuben get Ursula out of the chair and into the backseat. Since most everything at the clinic was well-worn and donated, the chair didn't have anything to identify it as theirs. Rather, it had the remnants of the Cedars-Sinai logo, as that prosperous hospital had handed the vehicle down to L.A. Central, which had passed it along to the clinic.

"How did a Cedars chair get down here?" the cop asked, mostly to himself.

"We got that cheap from my in-home care. I don't think they stole it," Ursula said, expertly redirecting the officer's investigative curiosity down another avenue of suspicion.

Once in the back seat of the patrol car and moving, the shotgun cop turned toward Ursula and Reuben, who were just finishing their burritos, and said, "You mind if we ask your names?"

"Is this about the wheelchair?" Ursula said with amusement.

"No ma'am. Just procedure."

"Of course, we understand. I'm Ursula Montanez, this is my grandson, Reuben."

"Thanks. By the way, did either of you notice a late-model, blue Toyota near the clinic?"

Reuben shook his head as Ursula said, "I can't tell one car from another. But I don't remember a blue car. Was there an accident or something?"

"It was stolen and we're looking for whoever took it. Probably one of the gangs," he said to Ursula. "We'll find out who snatched it soon enough. The gangs steal the cars then take them apart or wipe them down in a garage somewhere, so they're not concerned about fingerprints. But, since they left this one, it's bound to have something that's in our system, unless it was part of an initiation for someone that's never been booked before. But that's not very likely."

The cop turned to Reuben about a half second after he had recomposed his face from the news that the cops would soon find his fingerprints all over the blue Toyota, "So, she's your grandmother?"

"Yes," he answered as flat as road kill. His mind had raced through all his school years trying to remember if he had ever been fingerprinted. He couldn't remember ever having to press his digits to an ink pad and then roll them over some piece of paper. So far so good, he thought, but he better not get busted for anything, or they'll have his ass in jail in a New York minute.

"I'm the Spanish *abuela*," Ursula cut in like a scalpel performing delicate surgery. "From the north, the Basque region near the French border. A little town called San Sebastian, do you know it?" Reuben was impressed with the woman's ability to think on her feet. He knew about the Basque, but wondered if such a town really existed. "His other grandparents were Mexican,

36

including my late husband Bernardo," she improvised with a transliteration of her second husband's name, which was the very white, very Jewish, Bernie Frank.

The polite interrogation brought Ursula and Reuben to the street outside Olivia Carillo's apartment building and, more importantly, seemed to satisfy the cops' curiosity. While the car idled, the shotgun cop and Reuben escorted Ursula up the steps to the main door of the building. Reuben handed over the keys so Ursula could find the right one for the front door, while he returned to the car with the cop to get the wheelchair, which he rolled over to the stoop in its collapsed position and then carried up the stairs to where Ursula was holding the door open. Both of them gave the police officers a wave as they entered the building.

They walked confidently over to the elevator and, when Reuben pressed the call button, the doors before them parted immediately. Like all elevator riders, they ascended to the fifth floor in silence. A placard let them know to turn to the right. When they found apartment 527, Ursula inserted a key in the lock and the door yielded. The light switch in the foyer was were it should be and gave off enough illumination for them to press ahead into the living room.

Suddenly, the adrenaline that had coursed through both fugitives for the last two hours drained from their bodies as if their feet and fingers were sieves. All the anxiety and stress of the night leaked out in invisible waves as they crumpled like abandoned marionettes, Ursula onto a small sofa, Reuben into an overstuffed chair that was either a very old family heirloom or a thrift store reject.

Chapter 10

Ursula and Reuben were sleeping the sleep of winter bears. Nothing short of a rock festival or a rocket attack was going to wake them. Complete exhaustion muffled the squeak of door hinges and tired foot falls that announced Olivia's arrival to her own apartment. That is, the apartment she shared with her grandmother, who was in Mexico for the week visiting relatives.

Despite her fatigue from working the graveyard shift, Olivia was ready to confront her nearly uninvited guests. But, their impenetrable slumber stripped Olivia of her pique and left her with only curiosity and the compassion she had developed working at the clinic.

As the first rays of morning light wormed their way under, around and through the partially-open blinds of the living room, Olivia lowered her bag lightly to the floor and walked slowly and quietly toward the bathroom strategically positioned between the apartment's two bedrooms. She almost hated to sit and relieve the pressure in her bladder, but nature could not be ignored. When she emerged from the bathroom, teeth brushed and face washed, she was glad to see that Reuben and Ursula had not stirred.

* * *

It was only three hours later when Olivia heard the toilet flush. Her first thought was that her own *abuela* had used the commercial break in one of her favorite *telenovas*, Spanish-language soap operas, to use the bathroom. Then it dawned on her that her grandmother was away, and half a heartbeat later, that the sound was from either Reuben or Ursula.

Olivia lay still and heard the sound of water running as someone washed their hands. She counted breaths waiting for the door to open . . . six, seven, eight. Living in small houses and apartments, she knew that almost no one took longer than seven breaths to dry their hands and emerge from a bathroom. Something wasn't right. If it was Reuben in the bathroom, he might be going through the medicine cabinet. Could he be looking for prescription drugs to steal? Had she put too much trust in him because he was Julian's brother? Or was he checking to see if she was taking birth control pills in the hope that . . . ? Why was she even thinking that? He was close to her in age, but still a bit younger, and she had never gone out with anyone who wasn't older—not that it would matter, she told herself.

But what if it was Ursula in there? Maybe she needed help, Olivia's compassionate clinic-working side took over. I should get up and see, she told herself, but was still worried it might be Reuben. As the fogginess of sleep was replaced with gaining cognizance, she realized all she had to do was go out into the living room and see which of them was still there.

Olivia swung out of bed in nothing but a knee-length T-shirt and took two steps toward the door before becoming aware of her semi nudity. She grabbed a faded yellow robe off the hook on her bedroom door and swung it on as she left for the living room. To her relief, Reuben was still crumpled up in the chair asleep, as only a teenager could do, though his position had changed some since she had come home.

On site of the boy, she reversed direction and tapped lightly on the bathroom door. "Ursula. *Abuela.* Are you alright? Do you need some help?"

There was a long pause before Ursula answered. "Is Reuben with you?"

"No, he's still asleep in the chair. Can I help you?"

"I need . . ."

"Yes, go on. What can I get you?"

"I hate to bother you . . ."

"Ursula," Olivia decided to use her soothing clinic voice. It invited trust but was direct so she could get down to business, "I understand that you may have a problem. I can help. I work with all kinds of stuff at the clinic."

"Can I borrow a bathrobe or something?"

Olivia understood Ursula's problem and embarrassment immediately. "Yes. I live here with my grandmother. I'll get you one of hers. Meanwhile, look under the sink, you might find something helpful there," she concluded, directing Ursula to where she could find her grandmother's Depends without having to ask directly.

Olivia found a rose-colored robe with sleeves down to the elbow and white lace trim, and squeezed it through the four-inch opening the elder woman allowed. In a trice, Ursula shuffled out of the bathroom; barefoot and robe-clad, though she still wore the white long-sleeve jersey she had donned the night before. Must be cold, despite the moderate temperature, Olivia thought. "I have to

39

do some wash later," she said, "I'll just throw your things in so you'll have clean clothes to go home in."

"Thank you, dear. I'll have to repay your grandmother for the, ah, . . ."

"Don't worry about it. She'll be glad to have helped."

"Where is she? Will she be back soon?"

"No, no. She's visiting relatives in Mexico. She won't be back for another week."

The women's chatter woke Reuben. He sat up straight as though he had slept soundly on a good mattress; no kinks, aches or stiffness—as only the young and athletic can enjoy, even if they slept in a sardine can. "Anybody using the bathroom?" he asked.

"No, go ahead, but don't take all day," Olivia said, wanting to use it next. She led Ursula to the small kitchen where the older woman sat at a modest wood table with four matching chairs. The two talked about the traveling grandmother, her trip to Mexico to visit with relatives and other generally safe subjects. Olivia got the big coffee can from the cupboard and spooned six cups of ground beans into the Mr. Coffee filter, added water and pressed the on button as Reuben entered the kitchen. "Be back in a minute," Olivia said as she moved quickly toward the bathroom.

Olivia reemerged a few minutes later, her hair brushed and tied back, the robe pulled tighter around her. The only sound was hot water bubbling up clear and steamy through the Mr. Coffee apparatus and dripping down hot and brown into the glass carafe releasing its rich, inviting smell into the kitchen.

Olivia pursed her lips together as she looked from Ursula to Reuben and back again, as the two sat at her and her grandmother's kitchen table. Then, quietly, without anger or accusation, she said, "I'd really like to know what is going on? Who are you? How did you end up at the clinic? And what's all this about a stolen car?"

Both of her guests were surprised by Olivia's calm, direct and authoritative tone. Both had been mentally spinning their own yarn of what they had been doing last night, why they were where they were, and how they came to be together. But their cobbled together stories fell to bits like a hurricane hitting a lumberyard. Her straightforward demeanor stripped away any pretense of deception and left them bare with only the truth on which to build a relationship with this stranger that rescued them both in their moment of need.

"Olivia," Ursula began first, "I want to thank you for everything you've done for me, and for Reuben here."

Erroneously sensing that Ursula was about to begin leading her down the proverbial garden path—to obfuscate and skirt a direct answer, she raised her otherwise controlled voice, "Listen old lady. I don't care if you are someone's grandmother. I've been working my ass off all night. I've only gotten about three hours sleep and I don't have time to mess with you. Don't give me any bullshit. I want straight answers or you can just get on down the road to your people. *Comprende!*"

Olivia expected to see shock on Ursula's face, if not for the accusation that she might lie, then for her tone of voice.

But it was Olivia and Reuben whose eyes shot open when the *abuela* looked up at her hostess and said in a calm, even tone, "Don't worry, young lady. You've been very kind and trusting and deserve to hear the truth. I have no intention of bullshitting around with you." Ursula waited two beats and then continued. "I actually know how to say that in four languages, five, if you count Yiddish. But I find it generally unnecessary, except to divert the conversation."

Olivia regained her composure and replied, "Would you like some coffee, *abuela*? Reuben?"

Chapter 11

Olivia puttered in the small kitchen for a few minutes to compose herself and her questions while the coffee brewed. She brought out three cups and a carton of milk, set them down on the old mahogany coffee table with its legs scarred from the vacuum and a few rings on the surface from sweaty beverage glasses. She went back to the kitchen and returned with a bowl of sugar and the carafe from the Mr. Coffee machine, which she set down on top of a *People en Español*, the Spanish-language edition of *People* magazine, to avoid more scarring on the table.

Reuben was now sitting up in the over-stuffed chair in which he had slept. Ursula was seated on the couch. Olivia noticed, as if for the first time, how shabby the old piece of furniture was, but her guests seemed to be quite comfortable. The younger woman sat down at the other end of the couch.

"Now, really, *abuela*. I want to know your story. But before you start," she continued, thinking about Ursula's problem in the bathroom, "do you need anything? Ya know, like blood pressure medicine, heart stuff, anything like that?"

"No honey. Thanks for asking but I'm not taking anything."

"Come on old lady. Someone your age, what, like 90 or something, not taking anything? You know I work at a clinic. And, I'm studying to be a nurse practitioner. There ain't no one your age without a prescription for something."

"You didn't ask if I had any prescriptions. You asked if I'm taking anything, and I'm not."

"You mean you're supposed to be taking stuff, but you aren't?" Olivia asked, incredulity lacing her question.

"That's pretty much it."

"What are you, crazy? If you need some medicine and stuff, and you aren't taking them, you could keel over and die."

"I guess so. But I decided not to take anything anymore. Besides, I haven't felt this good since I moved back here. But thanks for your concern."

"Doesn't that scare you?" Reuben chimed in.

"No honey. Not in the least. I've lived through much worse than what happened last night."

"I doubt that," Reuben said. "What do white people know about bad stuff, eh? You ain't never lived in South Central. People here either can't get a job or can't get one that's worth a shi. . . a da. . . a dime. Whole families are crammed into small apartments. Moms working two jobs to raise their kids. No one getting any doctoring. No one getting any richer. Kids getting killed," he continued as his voice dropped down to a near whisper, "brothers getting killed. What do you know about stuff like that?"

"Actually, quite a bit," Ursula said quietly, comfortingly. "Would you like to hear about that, or about what I'm up to now?"

"I dunno," Reuben answered dejectedly.

"How about both *abuela*?" Olivia said.

* * *

"First. I'm not 90. I'm 87 years old. That's pretty close to 90, but a lot can happen in three years. There could be another senseless war. There will be a new president. And it's almost certain that there will be more pain and suffering. "I was born in 1920 in Berlin."

"You gonna tell us your whole life story *abuela*?" Olivia asked.

"Just the highlights, or the lowlights, depending on how you look at it. You two can judge for yourselves. But it's important to know that whatever happened, I'm here now, in pretty good shape, considering, and I really shouldn't complain, though I have and will. Is that okay with the two of you?"

"I guess so," said Reuben.

"If it doesn't take, like a month," Olivia answered. "I've got a job and nursing school, and I gotta sleep sometime."

They all laughed a little at that, and relaxed a bit as Ursula began.

"The first twelve years of my life were a lot like all the other kids who grew up in an upper-middle class home in most western countries. There was a depression going on, mostly thanks to World War I and a lot of greed in stock markets worldwide. Lots of people were out of work, especially in Germany, because we lost that one, too. But my family wasn't as bad off as some because my father had a clothing business. He made a lot of money during the war making uniforms for the German army.

"After the war, he switched his shop to making uniforms for other groups like policemen, firemen, hospital workers and such. He had a half-dozen people working with him, so we were comfortable, but not rich.

"I did well in school. The teachers liked me and I had a lot of friends. That is, until January, 1933."

"Why? What happened then?" Reuben asked.

"That was when Adolph Hitler became chancellor of Germany. Overnight, my favorite teacher let me know that she was a Nazi, and that I was nothing. Even my friends stopped talking to me."

"So, you're Jewish," Olivia said.

"Of course, honey. And, just because I am Jewish, along with my Jewish classmates, I was suddenly trash, left out of playtime, left out of learning, the butt of jokes and jeers, and bullied, even though I was the same person I had been the day before. But because of my family's religion, I was ostracized, made to feel that I didn't belong. That I was less of a person than my classmates."

"Like being a Mexican in the United States, huh?" said Reuben.

"I'm sure that it is very similar," Ursula continued. "My father's business disappeared overnight. Orders for uniforms got canceled. One by one, he had to lay off his workers, all Jewish tailors, poor things, they could barely scratch out a living. They could only do work for or sell to other Jews. They couldn't buy new materials, they had to work with second-hand fabrics, rags even. It was all my father could do to hold onto his shop. Just doing mending and altering for the few customers who would come to see him, Jews and a few brave Gentiles for whom he had done work for years.

"In about a year we went from having meat and eggs and good bread in the house to eating watery stew that was mostly cabbage and potatoes; from being able to buy new, fashionable clothes to wearing *schmattas*, rags; threadbare dresses and sweaters that had patches on their patches; from being able to go out onto the street or to the park, to practically hiding in our house all day."

"Really?" Olivia questioned.

"Well, maybe it took more than a year, but yes, it seemed we went from accepted and respected members of our community to pariahs in a very short time."

"Pariahs?" asked Reuben.

"Outcasts," Ursula said as she watched Reuben silently mouth the word as he committed it to memory. Smart boy, she thought, as she continued her story. "To make matters worse, Father went to work one morning to find the word *Jude* painted on the door and Nazi swastikas on both windows. *Jude* means Jew in German. It was the Nazis' way of telling people not to do business with Papa.

"He and Mama scrubbed the offending marks off the windows. The next morning, he found both windows broken."

"Was that the Crystal Night?" Olivia asked.

"No, that came later, in 1938. In German that is one word, *Kristallnacht*, it means night of broken glass. This was just the local gang of hooligans making trouble." Both Reuben's and Olivia's eyes widened when Ursula mentioned gangs.

"What did he do then?" Reuben asked. "Did he call the police?"

"Oh no. He couldn't do that. The police were rapidly becoming members of the Nazi Party. They were as bad as the gangs. They would beat Jews and anybody else the Nazis were against with no repercussions. If anyone fought back, they would arrest them and, sometimes people would just disappear."

"They hurt other people besides the Jews?" Reuben asked, "like who?"

"Gypsies, communists, intellectuals, artists, homosexuals, Catholics, Masons, people with disabilities, other religious orders and anyone who helped Jews or the others they targeted."

"What about Hispanics and blacks?" Reuben said.

"There weren't any Mexicans or blacks living in Germany then. The only Hispanics they might have known were the Spanish, and they were allies of the Nazis. But I'm sure they wouldn't have liked Mexicans, blacks, Muslims, Mormons and a long list of others. In fact, half of the twelve million people that perished in their camps were Jews, the other half were killed for other beliefs or reasons."

"What did your father do then? Could they live on your mother's salary?" Olivia asked.

"My mother didn't work then. Most women, especially married women, didn't have jobs then. They took care of the house and the children. But they did contribute what they could, especially making sure the kids got an education—that has always been a major part of being Jewish. Mothers were in charge of early education, kindergarten comes from a German word meaning a garden for children. A garden where kids were nourished with

45

knowledge, where they would start to learn about their world, maybe some early reading and counting, and always something about their religion. My father always used to say, 'Get a good education. Someone can steal your money or your home. You can lose your spouse, your family and your friends. But no one can take away your education. And as long as you have that, you can make your way in the world.' Of course, that is what all Jewish fathers, and Jewish mothers, tell their children. Probably for thousands of years.

"It's also why Muslims used to refer to Jews as 'The people of the book.' They meant the bible, or the Torah, the first five books of the bible that every Jewish child learned from.

"Anyway, my parents made sure that my brother, Walter—who was 10 at the time, and I, understood what was happening. That it wasn't our fault. That we couldn't just stay where we were and wait for the Nazis to come and take us away. They started making plans to come to the United States. Mama had a half sister here she wrote to.

"Like today, the U.S. didn't just let anyone in. We needed a sponsor and we needed to be part of the quota of Jews, and/or Germans, who they would let immigrate."

Reuben and Olivia were settled in, rapt with attention, waiting for Ursula to tell them about coming to the United States. Then, Reuben's cell phone rang, shattering the moment like *Kristallnacht*.

Reuben looked at the caller I.D. and quickly pressed a button and said, "*Hola, mama.*" In Spanish he continued to tell her that he had overslept. Yes, he knew it was Friday, and that he was late for school, he was looking down at his tennis shoes. Yes, he was sorry, he assured her as he looked up and caught Ursula motioning to him for the phone.

Reuben asked his mother to hold a moment, "*por favor, por favor,*" he entreated her two more times before she stopped her scolding long enough for him to hand the phone to Ursula.

"*Hola señora Montanez,*" Ursula began. "*Yo soy Ursula Carillo,*" she said, borrowing Olivia's last name. In Spanish she went on to explain that Reuben had come home with her daughter, Olivia—a friend of her late son, Julian—and was going to sleep on the couch. Then Ursula told her, "I fell in the bathroom and Olivia and Reuben took me to the clinic to make sure I wasn't seriously injured."

46

As Ursula was spinning her yarn Reuben was again impressed by the elderly woman's memory and, as she had advised him earlier, her ability to tell enough truth to be credible, and enough lie so his mother wouldn't ask a lot of questions.

"Anyway," Ursula had slipped into English, "it's all my fault that Reuben overslept. I'll have him out of here in two minutes so he can come home and change before going to school. *Lo siento mucho*," she interjected an apology in Spanish and then continued in that language, "I do hope you'll let him come back over later, he is a very sweet boy, I don't know what I would have done last night without his help."

Ursula had assured Reuben that she would wait for him to return in the afternoon to finish her story. "Besides," she said, "Olivia and I need our beauty rest. Well, at least I do."

Chapter 12

Although Olivia and Ursula expected Reuben to be back in the late afternoon, it was already getting dark when he rang the bell from downstairs. Olivia buzzed him in as Ursula was busy in the kitchen. She had sent Olivia out to the *bodega* to pick up some black beans and shrimp so she could make them Cuban-style *camarones* for dinner—marinated shrimp sautéed with tomatoes, ginger, garlic and pepper served over white rice and black beans. The smells brought back memories of her early freedom from oppression. It also made her long for a cold mojito or at least a margarita; even though the latter was distinctly Mexican and contemporary.

"Oh, I haven't made food like this in 50 years," Ursula was saying when she heard the buzzer. "I hope you kids like it," she called after Olivia, "mine didn't care much for it; they prefer Taco Bell and Chipotle to the real thing."

"Reuben, what's wrong?" Olivia said when she opened the door. The young man looked like he had been in a scuffle. His hair was tousled, he had a red abrasion on his right cheek, and the Montanez baseball jersey he wore open over a navy blue T-shirt had a tear on one sleeve.

"It's nothing," he said, with typical teenage dejection.

"Bullshit," Olivia challenged. "Come into the bathroom, let me have a look at your face. Did you get hit anywhere else?"

"I didn't get hit."

"Don't give me that. I know the signs of a fight when I see them. Now tell me, did you get hit anywhere else? Stomach? Ribs? Kidneys? Kicked in the balls?" Reuben blushed at the mention of his genitals. "Don't blush, stupid. This is serious. And don't lie."

"I took a couple to the ribs. And my shirt got torn."

"Take off both shirts, I want to see." He obeyed her instructions. She checked his ribs and back. "You're okay here," she said, tacitly admiring his trim, well-muscled frame. "Let me put something on your face. It's just a little Neosporin with a pain killer. It'll take away some of the heat and stop any infection in the little scrapes on your cheekbone. Put your T-shirt back on, we'll take care of the baseball jersey after dinner."

Ursula listened approvingly to Olivia's instructions from her duties in the kitchen. Her mothering instincts made her want to take over, but her hostess had plenty of experience and was at least

48

a professional in training. Besides, Ursula wanted the dinner she was cooking to be perfect, as much for herself as for the kids.

Olivia sat Reuben down at the oak dining room table. It had four chairs but one of them was pressed almost to the wall to make more room in the small vestibule for the table and the other three chairs.

Ursula could see Reuben clearly from her post in the kitchen. "*Boychik*," she called to him in affectionate Yiddish, then, "*Hijo*. So, tell me what happened already? You can't just show up here looking like something the cat dragged in," she exaggerated, "without us noticing."

"It's nothing, *abuela*. Whatcha cooking in there?"

"*Camarones*, Cuban style. Well, I'm cooking the beans and rice. Don't want to start the shrimp too early, they cook up in minutes."

"Sounds good. When can we eat?"

Boys! Ursula and Olivia thought, though Olivia wasn't much older herself. "After you tell us what happened," Ursula said, figuring she could at least extort the story.

"But I'm starving," he replied. "And the smells aren't making it any easier."

"You start talking, I'll start cooking the main dish. Okay, *hijo*?"

"Fair enough," he said. Ursula checked the beans and the rice and started the flame on another burner. She scraped chopped tomatoes from the cutting board into a cast iron frying pan to reduce the juices. She would add the shrimp marinade, which had the finely chopped garlic, grated fresh ginger and fresh ground pepper in a suspension of cheap red wine and virgin olive oil, reduce the sauce and then save the shrimp for last. They would sauté for five to seven minutes—Ursula never timed them, she knew when they were done by their color—and then serve the *camarones* over a bed of white rice mixed with black beans that had simmered with minced garlic, basil and a few pinches of salt. Somewhere along the way she had added chopped scallions to the rice, but no one knew exactly when. Olivia had already made up a salad.

As the older woman worked her magic, Reuben let his head drop so he was staring at the floor, then said, "It was Marco."

"Who's Marco?" Ursula asked.

49

"He's the guy you were with last night from the *Diecinueves*," Olivia said, "isn't he?"

"What's the *Diecinueves*?" Ursula asked.

Reuben was silent.

"Well?" Olivia said to Reuben, "it's not my gang. You better tell her about it, *hombre*."

Reuben raised his head and began, "Marco's a friend of mine from school. Well, that is, I met him in school. But he's not there anymore."

"Why's that?" Ursula asked, thinking her motherly tone might be more effective than Olivia's scorn.

"Well, he kinda dropped out."

"Kinda dropped out?" Olivia challenged, and then caught a reproving look from Ursula. "I mean, what happened?"

Reuben realized he couldn't lie to these ladies. They had already done so much for him. Either of them could have pointed the police right to him. He could be down in county jail right now eating dry toast with mystery meat and phlegm-like gravy, instead of sitting in a nice old apartment waiting to eat Cuban-style shrimp.

"I guess I kinda wanted to be like Marco. Well, not like him, but to have the shi… stuff he has. You know, cool shoes and threads, a fancy smartphone, chicks," he blushed as he looked back at the floor, the only place from where he sat where he could avoid the looks of disappointment from the women.

"Anyway, he dropped out of school to spend more time with the *Diecinueves*."

"What does nineteenth have to do with anything?" Ursula asked.

"It's short for Nineteenth Street gang," Olivia said.

"So, what does that mean? Do they live there or something?"

"No one remembers how they got their name," Olivia said. "They've been here forever, well at least as long as my family's been here, and that goes back about 60 years."

"There's one guy who said the gang is over a 100 years old," Reuben said, hoping to change the focus of the conversation.

"Really?" Ursula said. "How can that be?"

"Whatever," Olivia drew them both back. "So why did Marco beat you up?"

" 'cause I fuc… messed up the initiation."

"Is that what last night was all about?" Olivia asked, "stealing a car to get into the gang?"

Ursula looked surprised and turned down the heat on her sauté and stood in the kitchen doorway, she wanted to hear about this.

"Essentially, yeah."

"And, how did you mess it up?" Ursula asked, a little sparkle of mischief in her eyes.

"We, that is, I, was supposed to hot-wire a car the gang picked out. Marco told me which one, and then he was supposed to be my lookout. But, instead of telling me someone was coming, he jumped Ursula—I'm sorry, *abuela*—and then he ran away.

"I thought he'd stay out of sight. Hang with the gang. But he came over to my house this morning after I had been there, changed, and went to school. My mother was really pissed."

"He didn't tell her about the gang, did he?" Olivia asked.

"No. He's stupid, but he ain't that stupid. He told her we were friends from school and he was just coming by to see how I was doing."

"She didn't buy that, did she?" Olivia asked.

"No way. She let him tell her his B.S. story. Thanked him for coming by. Told him I was in school. And then she called in sick on her day job so she would be home when I got there."

"But why do you think your *madre* didn't believe Marco?" Olivia asked.

"Marco got tats," he said, then turned toward the kitchen doorway, "that's tattoos, *abuela*. He's got some on his arms and a really big one of the Virgin of Guadalupe on his back. You can see the light stuff over her head on his neck. She didn't know it was the Virgin, and she didn't care to hear about it when I tried to explain. She just reamed me out for hanging around with gang *mierda*, and my mother doesn't swear.

"She was really going strong. She yelled a lot. Told me I was a disappointment to her and our priest. Why did I think she worked two jobs? And all that stuff. I tried to tell her that I was getting good grades and should be able to have a good time and to pick my own friends, but that made her even more mad. Then she told me that she was glad Julian wasn't here to see this. That he had sacrificed so much for me, like Jesus, she said, he even died for you."

"Oh my God," Ursula said. She took two steps from the kitchen doorway toward Reuben and wrapped her translucent white arms around his shoulders. "*Hijo*. Reuben. It's going to be all right," she said as he burst into tears. Olivia watched, wondering how Ursula had known what Reuben was feeling. "She's just really mad, *hijo*. As much with herself as she is with you. She will get over it. She will forgive you. And she will pray to your late brother to forgive you, too. And he will. But you have to help."

"I tried, *abuela*. I really tried. I grabbed Julian's baseball shirt and ran out of the house. I went and found Marco. I told him what a jerk he was. That he was stupid for coming to my home. That he was an asshole for upsetting my mother. I wanted him to apologize. But he just yelled that I was a little *puta*–sorry. That I had fuc. . . ah, messed up my initiation and that I would never be good enough to be in the *Diecinueves*. That my brother was another *puta* who didn't have the balls to be in the *Diecinueves*. So I ran at him with my fists swinging, just trying to give him as much hurt as I felt."

"Did you nail the little bastard?" Ursula asked, to the surprise of both Reuben and Olivia.

"I'm pretty sure I got in a few good punches," he said with a grin. "The last time I saw his face, his nose was bleeding and there was redness on his cheek, right under his left eye."

"Good for you," Ursula said.

"Yeah, sure." Reuben said, "But then three of his *Diecinueves* buddies jumped me. All I could do was push them away and run like a scared rabbit."

"That was a smart thing to do," Olivia said. "They would have kicked your butt from Hope Street all the way to the clinic, if not some ER. You just showed them that you're smarter than they are."

"Really, you think so?"

"She's right," Ursula said. "When you're outnumbered and outgunned, you need to remember that it's better to run away so you can fight again another day."

Reuben smiled and looked from Ursula to Olivia who said, "I knew Julian. He would have been really proud of you today, standing up for your mother, telling that gang *mierda* what you think of them. "Have you talked to your mom since you left?"

"No, I should call her, huh?"

Ursula had loosened up her hold when Reuben stopped crying, but she was still close enough to give him a gentle slap up the back of his head, "What do you think?"

"What should I say?"

"First, tell her you're sorry. Then," Ursula paused and looked at Olivia. The younger woman read her mind and nodded, "then, tell her where you are and ask her if it's okay to spend another night." Reuben beamed as he reached for his phone. "I'll be glad to talk to her again if she wants," Ursula said.

Chapter 13

"Ursula, that was delicious," Olivia said after the trio had finished dinner.

"Your salad was good, too," Reuben said, perhaps a little too enthusiastically. But both women merely accepted their compliments without any false modesty.

"Well," Ursula said, "I guess there's just one more thing left to do." Reuben thought she was going to clear the table and continue her story. But both women stayed in their chairs and looked at him.

"Oh yeah," he said, the light of clarity nearly visible behind his eyes. "Please, let me clean, you both made such a wonderful meal." The ladies laughed, and Reuben joined in even before the blush left his face. He quickly gathered up the dishes and headed for the kitchen. There wasn't much, so he made quick work of soaping them down, rinsing them off and placing them in the drying rack.

"Reuben," Olivia said, "do you know how to take care of a cast iron pan?"

"I was just going to wash it in the left over water."

"No, no," she said softly, "let me do it." She squeezed in beside him and took the heavy skillet from his hands. "You just wipe out whatever had collected, give it a little scrubbing if it needs it, but never use detergent. Give it a good rinse with plain water," she talked as she worked, "give it a shake and then put it back on the burner on high for a minute or so to dry it without rusting. If it looks too dry, like this here," she pointed to a whitish spot in the black pan, then it needs to be seasoned."

"You put salt and pepper and stuff on it?"

"No silly," she said, noticing that Ursula was stifling a snicker. "You put a tablespoon or two of vegetable oil in the pan and heat it on high for another minute. That expands the iron and lets the oil seep in so stuff won't stick to it. If it's a brand new pan," she continued, realizing what a novice he was in the kitchen, "you put in an inch of oil and heat it in the oven at 350 degrees for about an hour."

"Wow, that sounds like a lot of work."

"It's nothing, *hijo*," Ursula chimed in. You don't have to watch it cook. You can do whatever you want while it's seasoning; read, check your email, Twitter, or whatever you kids do."

"You Tweet on Twitter," Reuben and Olivia said at the same time reflexively.

"Thank you both," she replied. "Now finish up in there. Can you make me some decaf coffee or some tea, Olivia? I'd like to sip while I finish answering your questions about my life."

Olivia put a kettle on the stove and got out a couple of cups and tea bags. "Reuben," she said, "some tea or something?"

"You got any Coke?"

"Sorry no, *mi abuela* has diabetes and I'm watching my weight. Water, juice, coffee or tea."

"Water's fine."

She brought him a glass and sat down, hoping Ursula wouldn't wait for her tea to continue. Her wish was granted.

"Okay. So, where did I leave off?"

"Your family was about to leave Germany and come to the U.S.," Reuben said.

"Well, not quite that fast. Some friend of my father and mother offered to let us stay at their house because other Jews were already being harassed by the brownshirts."

"Brownshirts?" Reuben asked.

"A gang of punks that intimidated Jews and others who opposed Hitler and the Nazi Party. Kind of like a militia. In fact, a lot like the neo-Nazi nuts playing 'war' with real guns and bombs in some parts of the U.S.," Ursula said.

"Yeah, a lot like the . . . ," Olivia cut herself off mid-sentence when she caught Ursula's disapproving glance. She wondered why the older woman didn't want her to say "gangs," but didn't want to second-guess her, figuring she could ask later.

"Anyway, we stayed with the Kurtzmans for three days before we could sneak aboard a train heading for Poland. It was a lot easier for Germans to get across the Polish border at that time, even Jews.

"It's a good thing we left our home when we did. On the second night we were with the Kurtzmans, someone threw a Molotov cocktail through the window of our living room. I don't know what would have happened if we had been there. Maybe we would have been able to put the fire out, maybe not. We'll never know."

"Did you go to Warsaw?" Olivia asked about the only city she had heard of in Poland as the teapot began to whistle.

"No. Warsaw is farther north and there were already too many Nazi sympathizers there," Ursula said as the younger woman went to the kitchen to pour. "We went to the town of Königsberg, where my father had some business associates," she continued as Olivia set the tea down on the dining room table. "They found him a job as a tailor, but there wasn't much work. My mother took on a job as a housekeeper, eventually working for a branch of the Rothschild family."

"The ones who make the wine?" Olivia asked.

"Yes," Ursula answered as she dunked her tea bag a couple of times and took a sip. "The Rothschilds also had banks in all the major countries in Europe and business interests around the world. Mother told me they were very nice to her, maybe because they were Jewish too, but mother thought they were like that with almost everyone.

"Anyway, we seemed to settle in well in Königsberg. The house was smaller than the one in Berlin, but the neighborhood was good, the school was good, and most people there spoke German as well as Polish. Father would travel up to Warsaw every few months to check on our applications to go to the United States. Of course, the situation got awkward dealing with the U.S. embassy in Poland trying to get papers to immigrate for a Jewish-German family. Father was very frustrated by the bureaucracy as well as the embassy people turning a blind eye to what was happening to German Jews. He told us that they were just a bunch of government incompetents who had their heads in the sand."

"I don't understand the Jews," Reuben said. "Why didn't you people do something? Why not fight the Nazis? Or at least, what did you say? 'Run away to fight another day'?"

"Some of us did. Some of us weren't so brave. Some weren't smart enough to see what was coming. They said, 'This can't happen. People will wake up and see what is going on. But, by the time that happened, it was too late for millions."

"What did they do? The ones who were brave?" Reuben asked with the enthusiasm only a teenage boy can have for fighting.

"We met another family in Königsberg, the Muellers. Their business was store window supplies and the father rescued a lot of Jewish people from Germany. Herr Mueller, that would be Mr. Miller in English. Anyway, he would drive across the border under the guise of a buying jaunt for his business. He would take either a male or female employee along, depending on whom he was to pick up. Once in Germany, the woman or man would leave and take a bus or train home. While going to Germany, Herr Mueller would have a good talk and joke with the border guard, and mention he was coming back late. So, whoever he picked up would pretend to be asleep. But the guard would remember the man from earlier, and wave him through. He did it for a long time, until it became too risky."

"Wow, that's really cool," Reuben said.

Olivia was about to say something but Ursula cut her off. "I guess in hindsight it is. But if Herr Mueller would have been caught, it would certainly have meant the concentration camps, and probably death, for his whole family. Would you think it was cool to fight Marco if meant that that gang of yours would come back and beat up your mother?"

"I never thought about it like that," Reuben said.

"It's okay, *hijo*," Ursula said. "It doesn't just take a very brave person to do something like that; it takes a cause that is so important that to live any other way would be intolerable.

"Anyway, we were able to stay in Königsberg for about three years before the cancer that was Nazi Germany began to make major inroads into the culture there. At first it was very subtle. The forced closure of *schuls*, Jewish schools, so the Jewish children would have to go to public schools where they could learn to read and write, but nothing about their religion or their heritage. In fact, Poland is such a Catholic country, that many public schools actually had morning prayers and lessons that emphasized Christianity.

"All of that was okay. It was good, in a way, to learn about that. It helped out later when we were in Cuba, also very Catholic at the time. And, it's always good to learn about other cultures. The more you do, the more similarities you will see, and less fear you will have.

"After closing the *schuls*, the temples were first restricted to only being open on the Sabbath, Saturday for Jews, and the high holidays. Then only the high holidays. Then closed until further notice. Then Jews were restricted from most hotels and restaurants, even from some shops. Imagine hating a people so much that you won't even take their money.

"You didn't need a crystal ball or the Internet to see what was going to happen next. Their newspapers printed the Nazi party

57

line. People talked with one another on the street and in the shops. Anyone who wanted to know, or needed to know what was going on, and what would happen next, could find out, especially if any of the Polish or other world leaders would have just taken the time to read *Mein Kampf*, and then taken it seriously."

"*Mein Kampf*?" Reuben said.

"It was Hitler's book about his life and what he planned to do as the leader of Germany, including taking over Czechoslovakia and Poland. So why that was a surprise to anyone in 1939 is beyond me. As my father said, 'government incompetents.'

"However, we're still in the early '30s. Anti-Semitism wasn't just creeping in by this time, it was a full-on march. My father made one last trip to Warsaw to try to get us immigration papers, and failed. A week later, we were back on the train. This time to Danzig."

"How did you learn to pronounce all those names?" Reuben asked.

"How did you learn to trill your Rs, like in burrito? You listen and really hear how something is said. Then you practice it in your head and finally you try it out on your tongue. I've seen you doing it. It's one reason I think you're too bright to waste you life in a gang. That and what you did for me."

Reuben blushed again, "Do you really think so?"

"Hey, enough about you," Olivia said good naturedly, "I want to hear more about Ursula's adventures."

"I'm afraid that's going to have to wait," said the older woman, "it's been a long day. I haven't cooked a meal like that in ages, much less eaten one. It's more tiring than I remember. I think I'd like to lie down for a while."

"You can use my grandmother's room," Olivia said. "The sheets are clean and I can wash them again before she comes back from Mexico."

"That's very nice of you, are you sure?"

"Of course. Why waste a perfectly comfortable and clean bed? Come on, I'll help you to the room."

"With one stop on the way?"

"Of course *abuela*, of course."

Chapter 14

Ursula's son Mike heard the combination of panic and anger in his sister Deborah's voice, "Why didn't you tell me you were going to take Mom for the weekend?"

"Huh? What?"

"Isn't she there? Come on Mike, don't fuck with me, let me talk to Mom."

"She's not here. Honest, Deb, I don't know what you're talking about."

"Mike, this is serious. Anna, the little Filipino girl at the home said Mom left Thursday night. It was about eight. She told me that Mom told her that she was spending a few days with you."

"She must have made a mistake. I wasn't even here on Thursday. I spent the night with Joyce. She's here now. We were going to go to the desert this weekend, but it's raining like hell there."

"I don't care about the weather in Palm Springs, damn-it, where's our mother?"

"Deb, calm down. I'm sure it's just some kind of screw up at the home. Do you want me to call there? I could drive over to check on her. But you're a lot closer."

"Fuck you. I'll go, as usual."

"Hey," he started to say, but the phone was already dead in his hand.

* * *

Officers Lincoln and Pascal were cruising their regular beat on Saturday morning noting the locations of the various gang members, merchants doing business, neighborhoods filled with people, dogs barking, cats prowling, and children doing their best to find some innocent mischief for their amusement, when the radio in the squad car crackled. "Prints on your stolen Toyota are in."

Pascal reached for the radio phone, "Yeah, whatcha got, Morrie?"

"Excluding the owner, some smudges that are probably anywhere from a few days to a couple of weeks old. We got near completes from two individuals that look fresh. A partial set on one fender that aren't in the system, at least not yet. Another set that looks like two full hand prints, fingers, thumbs, even palms, on a rear door. Those belong to a little punk from the *Diecinueves*

59

named Marco Lopez. Real easy to I.D. too. He's five-seven, 155, brown hair and eyes, ink on both arms, and the Virgin of Guadalupe on his back."

"Now if we could just get these home boys to run around shirtless for a few hours, we can find him in no time," said Pascal

"Might not be that bad. The fucking thing's so big you can see the light rays from her halo going up the kid's neck," Morrie told him.

* * *

Despite an impulse to run to the desert with his newest girlfriend and avoid any emotional involvement, Mike got into his BMW and headed to the Valley. When he arrived at the retirement home he found his sister in the spacious lobby haranguing the mostly Filipino staff. He looked around at the septuagenarians, octogenarians and nonagenarians shuffling about or sitting in semi-vegetative states, and recalled with cowardly clarity why he hardly ever visited. And, why their mother wanted to stay with her friends in Arizona. Of course, he had to concede, the healthier, more active inmates were probably out and about, shopping, going to a movie, visiting friends and family; or hiding from them, like Ursula.

Sensing his arrival, Deborah whirled around on one fashionably-stacked heel that helped accentuate her legs all the way up to the bottom of her shorts. "I thought you and Barbie *du jour* were heading for the desert?"

"It's Joyce. I thought you liked her?"

"Never mind, this isn't about you. It's about Mom. The police are on their way. It's been almost 48 hours. That makes it an official missing person."

"It being Mom?"

"Fuck you," she said. Mike turned to leave. "Not so fast buster," Deborah continued. "You wait here until they arrive. Doubtful as it may seem, you might be able to add something that will help."

They tolerated each other in silence for the next few minutes until a squad car from the L.A.P.D. pulled up. Although the retirement home was in Encino, it was still part of the greater Los Angels megalopolis. And, although every attempt was made to coordinate activities among the various police sub-stations around the ginormously, over-populated area generically referred to as Los Angeles, some things just never crossed the barriers imposed by the racial, religious and socio-economic differences between rival jurisdictions. However, Deborah and Mike didn't know this.

Sergeant Gallagher was first through the double glass doors. He was followed immediately by Officer Swarzen. It didn't take them long to be brought up to speed. The four of them, Deborah, Mike, Gallagher and Swarzen were accompanied to Ursula's room with the last caregiver to have seen her, Carmelita. Ursula's room was neat and tidy. Her toothbrush, hairbrush, prescriptions and other essentials were all in their appropriate places in the oversized bathroom. The entire situation had the appearance that the room's occupant had gone out for a stroll, was visiting friends in the building, or had just gone down to the dining room on the main level.

"It doesn't make our job any easier," Swarzen said in her kindest manner. "But the good news is there's no sign of a struggle or accident. So we can assume that your mother is probably all right. Sometimes older people just wander off."

"My mother wouldn't do that," Deborah said, ignoring that Ursula was Mike's mother, too. "She'd call to let me know where she was going. There was nothing wrong with her brain. She didn't just wander off."

"What are these prescriptions for?" Gallagher asked noting several bottles in a drawer in the bathroom.

"Ah, the usual things, blood pressure, ah . . ." Deborah's voice trailed off.

"She was taking pills for hypertension and a blood thinner," Carmelita said, "also for her cholesterol, medicine for her kidneys, something to help her sleep, she had acid reflux, back and leg pain, occasional incontinence and a slight heart murmur. Except for blood clots, none of her problems are really bad by themselves, just inconvenient and annoying. But, when you put them all together, along with her loss of hearing and the beginnings of macular degeneration, well, some days she also needed an antidepressant, too."

"Did you know about all that?" Mike asked Deborah.

"Well, of course," Deborah said with a strong, definitive voice, trying to bluff her way through her ignorance. "I've been taking care of her since she moved back to California. You'd know about her condition too, if you ever spent any time with her."

Mike was about to answer his sister in no uncertain terms, but was cut off by the female officer. "We'll put out a bulletin for our officers to be on the watch for your mother," Swarzen said. "Officer Gallagher and I will drive the area ourselves, talk with shop owners and restaurant people to see if anyone's seen her. She has to eat and use the bathroom. Someone, someplace, must have seen her. We'll also check bus drivers along the major streets and cab companies that serve the area."

* * *

Officers Lincoln and Pascal were cruising the neighborhood where Olivia Carillo, her real grandmother, Reuben Montanez and the gang known as the *Diecinueves*, lived. And where Ursula Frank was staying temporarily under the assumed identity of Reuben's grandmother, or *abuela*, as one is known in Spanish.

Various images lit up the laptop computer that was secured to their patrol car's dashboard. There were rotating images that filled the screen with the license plate numbers of stolen vehicles, and mug shots of various nefarious individuals the L.A.P.D. and other law enforcement agencies were interested in locating, including a *Diecinueves* gang member named Marco Lopez, who Lincoln and Pascal took a particular interest in.

There was also the occasional missing person, including a photo of a smiling Ursula Frank from her 75th birthday, with the rest of the family inexpertly cropped out. She was wearing a smart navy blue jacket over a stylish pink rayon-silk blend blouse. Her hair was immaculately coifed, her makeup masterfully applied to take another ten years off her appearance, and her glasses sported black plastic frames. On close examination, the picture bore a passing resemblance to the woman in the wheelchair the officers escorted home the other night with her "grandson."

However, neither Officer Lincoln nor Officer Pascal gave the picture of the missing woman from way out in the Valley a close examination. And the photo soon dissolved into a real-time video of another of L.A.'s inconsequential slow car "chases" down I-10 that was coming in from a network news helicopter feed.

The screen wouldn't have held the officers' attention for long anyway, as they wheeled slowly up to a group of Latinos hanging around a mom-and-pop *bodega*. On the edge of the group, a young man in a T-shirt and baggy jeans slouched at approximately five-foot-six or -seven. His black hair was cut short on the sides and back, revealing the upward streaming lines of a

62

tattoo; possibly the radiating halo of the Virgin of Guadalupe. Like his companions, the youth had a black and red bandana, the sign that they were members of the *Diecinueves*. Two were tied about the neck, three were fashioned into do-rags, Marco's just hung limp from his hip pocket, which also housed his right hand.

The squad car eased up next to a curb painted red for the purpose of accessing a fire hydrant. Both officers lighted from the car with confident caution. They approached the half-dozen young men who met their gaze with practiced indifference.

"We're looking for Marco Lopez," Pascal said, her right hand steady on the holstered stun gun she wore on the opposite hip from her service piece.

"Why you wanna know?" asked the tallest of the gang members.

"His mother said playtime is over and she wants him to come home," Lincoln said.

At the mention of his mother, Marco flinched involuntarily. It was just enough for Lincoln to grab Marco's right wrist, yank it out of his pocket and pull it up between his shoulder blades. In the next instant, Pascal pulled handcuffs from her belt and locked them into place on Marco's left wrist. She left them to dangle so she could pull her stun gun, which she let hang in her right hand at her side—it was all the intimidation she needed. Lincoln lowered Marco's right arm and locked the loose end of the handcuffs around his wrist.

"Marco Lopez," Pascal addressed the young man while keeping her eyes on the other five gang members, "we're taking you in for grand theft auto." She then read him his Miranda rights and put her hand over his head as Lincoln coaxed Marco's body into the back of the squad car.

* * *

Convinced that Ursula Frank had just wandered off in a state of semi-dementia, despite what her daughter Deborah had said, Officers Gallagher and Swarzen didn't give their missing person problem a great deal of attention. As promised, they did circulate the picture they had of the older woman to the RTD, the cab companies that served the area, and even checked with personnel at a dozen local shops that would have been open Thursday night, and another half-dozen restaurants. Although one or two people in the neighborhood recognized her, despite the age of the photo and the makeup job, no one remembered seeing her recently.

One cab driver who was supposed to pick up a fare at the nursing home told his dispatcher that she looked familiar. "Perhaps," he had said, "she was nearby where he stopped for a fare that never showed up," but he couldn't be positive.

"Where did your cabby go from the nursing home?" Swarzen asked the dispatcher on her cell phone.

"He had been on shift since 6:00 a.m.," the dispatcher answered. "He decided to call it a night and deadheaded it home, across town."

"Where across town?" she asked, making sure not to leave any loose ends that might reflect poorly on the investigation.

"Just east of downtown."

"That's quite a schlepp."

"Yeah. You can't blame the guy for chucking it, it's almost an hour drive at that time of night. He's off for a few days. You want his address?"

"Sure," she replied, writing it down but knowing there was no way in hell she was going to chase all the way downtown to question someone who *may* have seen a woman who bore a resemblance to Ursula Frank.

* * *

Officers Lincoln and Pascal had barely pulled out of earshot of the other gang members when Marco Lopez began to rat out Reuben. "This kid, his name's Reuben Montanez. He was the one that stole that car. Really, it was his idea. He wanted to prove he was good enough to be in the *Diecinueves*. He gave me fifty bucks to be a watch for him."

"You realize that you have been read your rights, Marco?" Pascal said.

"Yeah, yeah. I know. But you got the wrong guy. I can show you where he lives. You can arrest him and let me go, huh? I didn't do nothin', I was just standing there, y'know. He broke into the car. He hot-wired it and drove it away."

"All by himself?" Lincoln said.

Marco remembered the old lady, but thought that would get him into more trouble. "Yeah, yeah. He was alone, man."

"So where did he take the car?" the office continued.

"I don't know. Wherever it was you found it."

"Why didn't he give it to the *Diecinueves*?"

64

"He probably got scared. Or, maybe he decided he was going to part it out or sell it himself."

"Is that what the *Diecinueves* do?"

"I don't know. I don't really know those guys. I guess. Maybe."

"You know Marco, that all sounds like a crock of shit to me," Pascal said. "Why don't you just shut up for now. We've got your prints on the car. It was obviously hot-wired and dumped. I think your best bet now is to shut the fuck up and wait for your public defender to cop a plea."

Both Lincoln and Pascal remembered the name Montanez. The pixilated old lady they had given a lift home the other night and her sweet grandson who was willing to push her wheelchair all the way from the clinic to their apartment. If only the perp in the back seat knew how ridiculous he sounded trying to implicate such an attentive and caring young man. Besides, they both thought to themselves, why should we go out of our way to find Montanez when we have a really tight case against this little punk?

Chapter 15

Olivia worked a short shift at the clinic on Saturday, and Reuben went home to do chores he had promised his mother would be done days earlier. The respite left Ursula to rest on her Shabbos, as God had intended. It also allowed her to organize her thoughts and save her strength, which she was beginning to feel might be waning.

Returning from their other obligations, Olivia and Reuben filled an hour or so with small talk, allowing the evening to end on a tranquil note. Olivia's guest, Ursula "Montanez," had been escorted to Olivia's real grandmother's bedroom where she seemed to fall asleep as soon as her head hit the pillow.

Olivia pulled out sheets, pillows and a blanket to make the living room sofa into a more comfortable bed for her other guest, Reuben Montanez. She was beginning to feel something for this kid who might have become a gang member by now, if not for his fortunate encounter with his adopted *abuela*. He was good-looking, like his late brother Julian. But were her feelings for Reuben, or the unrequited feelings she might have had for Julian? She did not know. Perhaps, she thought, she was just really, really tired. And maybe a bit horny, too.

"Good night, Reuben," she said rather formally. And, then softened enough to give him a hug that sent a spark of want through both their hormone-filled, late-teen bodies. Pulling back she said, "How old are you anyway?"

"Almost eighteen."

"Almost?"

"Two-and-a-half months. Why?"

"Oh, just curious."

* * *

The familiar smell of coffee wafted along the sun's rays and crept under the bedroom doors to awaken Olivia and Ursula. Each thought the other had gotten up and started breakfast. And each was equally pleased and surprised to find Reuben in the kitchen laying strips of bacon into the cast iron frying pan. Bread was waiting to be toasted, butter and jam were on the table, and an open egg carton was on the counter next to the stove.

"*Hijo. Qué es esto?*" Ursula smiled.

66

"I've been cooking Sunday breakfast for *mi madre* since my brother died. Of course, we would do it earlier so we wouldn't miss mass."

"I'm sorry, Reuben," Ursula said more seriously. "I didn't realize . . ."

"It's okay. She said it was all right to spend the night, so she knew what she was getting into," he smiled. "I'm sure she'll be fine this once."

"Okay," Olivia said, "Reuben's got breakfast under control. How about I pour us some coffees and you tell us what happened after you left, ah . . . how do you say it?"

"Königsberg," Reuben said, though not as nasally as a German or a Pole.

"Excellent, Reuben. Yes, from Königsberg we moved to Danzig, which is now called Gdansk, another part of Poland.

"I've heard of that," Olivia said.

"Indeed. It's up north on the Baltic Sea, making it a prime shipping port for whatever country controls it. Before and after the war, that was Poland. But, of course, the Nazis wanted it for Germany. It is also where Lech Walesa, probably Poland's best known president, was born and came to fame.

"Anyway, Danzig or Gdansk. If you can believe it, our apartment was even smaller. Just one bedroom. My brother Walter and I had to sleep on a daybed in what was the living room and dining room."

"Like this place?" Reuben said. Olivia blushed embarrassment.

"No, *hijo*. Smaller. This apartment is luxurious by comparison. Here there are two bedrooms and a full, private bath. There it was only the one bedroom, no division between the living room and dining room. Where the table was, that was the dining room. Where the daybed was, that was the living room. And the toilet and bathtub were down the hall."

"For the four of you?" Olivia asked.

"Yes. It made it very difficult to have any friends over. But it was the only place we could find that we could afford, and where people would rent to us."

"Because you were Jews?" Reuben said.

"Yes. But we only stayed there about a year. It was now 1935 or 1936. Hitler convinced the International Olympic Committee to hold the games in Berlin."

"That would be 1936," Reuben said.

"Yes. Of course, 1936. So he could show the world what magnificent athletes his blonde-haired, blue-eyed, Christian Aryans were."

"And that was when Jesse Owens got four gold medals. He kicked their Nazi asses," Reuben said proudly. Then to Olivia, "And he was black."

"I knew that," Olivia said, giving Reuben an affectionate punch to his arm.

"Yes. But I think all that just made Hitler even more mad. To show the world how tough he was, he had legions of soldiers that marched down wide boulevards, filling them from sidewalk to sidewalk with goose-stepping men in impressive uniforms as far as the eye could see. He and his propaganda machine made sure the whole spectacle was filmed for the world to see.

"We all knew that it was just a matter of time before he would send those troops into battle. To take Czechoslovakia, Poland and more. We also knew that he would be rounding up Jews along his march and getting rid of them. 'The Final Solution,' Heinrich Himmler, one of Hitler's advisors, called it."

"Jesus. That's worse than being a Mexican here," Reuben said.

"In all honesty, you can't really compare the two," Ursula said. "'The Final Solution' was the work of a madman and a handful of opportunistic cronies who stole everything they could from the Jews: property, dignity, the ability to make a living and, finally, their lives.

"But, that doesn't mean that what is happening to Mexicans, Asians, Muslims, Native Americans, and other people of color is any less demeaning or damaging than what the Nazis did to Jews. It just means that there is no obvious, systematic, planned scheme in place to actually take away your home, all of your possessions and to wipe out your entire population. There is just a subtle undercurrent designed to keep some people from advancing or getting too much influence.

"Watch out for that children. Don't let it happen. Make something of yourselves. There are both male and female black or brown mayors, even a black president. It may be harder for you than a white kid, but don't let other people define who are. And the best way to do that is to get a good education and a good job in a field that our society needs."

"Like a lawyer or a doctor?" Olivia asked.

"Only if that's what you really want. The world really doesn't need another lawyer, though we can use more doctors who will go where the need is greatest. But there's nothing wrong with being a carpenter, bus driver, painter or plumber. Society needs people who can keep things running smoothly. They always will, so there is a good living to be made there."

"What about a car thief?" Olivia asked, giving Reuben another jibe.

"A good car thief might also be an excellent mechanic. An excellent mechanic can choose to specialize in Lexus, Mercedes or Cadillacs, and make a damn good living doing it."

Reuben smiled and returned Olivia's punch.

"But, back to Gdansk," Ursula said with a moment of joy, and then her voice dropped. "It was Berlin and Königsberg all over again. More and more people looked at us with distain. Fewer and fewer places were open to us. It seemed nobody welcomed us or even the little money we had. I was 17, but I still remembered when I was ten years old and got a new pair of shoes whenever my old ones were worn. Now I hadn't had a new pair of shoes in almost eighteen months. Luckily, I had stopped growing. So, my shoes still fit, but they needed mending. Father traded some tailoring work with a Jewish shoemaker. All the Jews had to make cutbacks on everything: housing, clothing, food. So my father stayed busy mending and taking in the worn suits and dresses of neighbors as the clothes got older and their owners got thinner. But they didn't have any money, so we were still dirt-poor. Besides, I don't think he would have taken much for his work. Our neighbors were no better off than ourselves. He would charge just enough to cover costs and maybe just enough more for a loaf of bread or a cabbage to help feed us.

"We knew we couldn't go on like that. We had given up hope of getting visas to the United States. Then, one of our neighbors told my mother she knew a way to get us to Holland where the King had refused to punish the Dutch Jews. But it required money to bribe policemen and for train fare.

"Without father's knowledge, mother sold the silver Shabbos candle holders she had gotten as a wedding present. She did it on a Sunday so there was time to make the necessary arrangements and get on the train to Amsterdam before Friday night, when she would have to light candles in them at sunset to celebrate the Sabbath.

"'Better we should welcome the Sabbath with freedom in a country where we're safe than to melt a little wax waiting for the rest of the world to understand what is happening here,' she said.

"Because of what should have been the usual expected delays, we didn't even get onto the train until Friday morning. That meant we would still be riding at sundown, which is against the laws of the Sabbath. But it also meant not letting father know about the silver Shabbos candle holders Mother had to sell for at least another week, because we couldn't possibly light candles on a train."

"What about celebrating the Sabbath?" Olivia asked.

"Fortunately for Jews, the Talmud, the commentary on the law—which starts with the Ten Commandments and includes the tradition of welcoming the Sabbath with the candle lighting—tells us that life is the most sacred of all things. Jews believe that in extreme cases, it is better to save a life than to blindly obey a law that would endanger that life. That is why even some orthodox doctors will work in a clinic on the Sabbath. Also, fortunately, it allowed the Israeli army to defend the country in 1973 when it was attacked on Yom Kippur, a very holy time for Jews.

"Sorry to keep digressing. We old people have a tendency to let our minds wander."

"It's no problem, *abuela*. Let me get you more coffee," Olivia said. "Please, go on. You said you were 17 and going to Holland. Did you have boyfriends?"

"Some things never change," Ursula said, the gleam back in her eyes. "Yes, believe it or not, I was a very pretty girl. There was interest from several young men, though I dare say, many of them wanted then what almost all men still want today, if you know what I mean."

Olivia nodded her understanding as Reuben tried to hide his blush behind a drink of coffee.

"Did you go out with them?" Olivia asked. "Do you know what happened to them?"

"There was one boy I liked a lot in Danzig. His name was Ees, short for Isaac. No one had any money to speak of, so we would walk along the beach or go to a park. Once, Ees and I got enough money together to buy just one ticket to the movies. I went in on the ticket and then, when the crowd began to grow inside and the ushers were busy, I opened the side door a few inches so Ees could sneak in. It made my heart race, I was so afraid I would get caught."

"So you were afraid you might get arrested?" Reuben asked.

"I was much more afraid of my father and what he would do. He had a way of just looking at you that made you feel like you were very small, a complete imbecile. It was worse than getting hit."

"So, you didn't get caught?" Reuben said.

"Not sneaking into the movies, but like any kid, there were times when I disappointed my parents, and my father made sure I suffered for it."

"Do you know what happened to Ees? Did he come to the U.S.? Did he ever get married?" Olivia asked.

The joy in Ursula's eyes was suddenly eclipsed by a murky cloud of sadness. "He said he wanted to marry me. He said that when this madness, the Nazis and all, was over, we would get married and move back to Berlin and have beautiful, smart children."

"And?"

"I told him I would marry him in the United States."

"So he came here?"

"No. He and his family stayed in Danzig when we left for Holland. They were still there when Hitler's troops invaded Poland. The entire family was sent to a concentration camp. His parents were gassed and burned in the ovens of Auschwitz. Ees and his sister Rose were young and strong. He got sent to the Russian front in 1945 to dig trenches for the Nazis. The Red Cross found him near Stalingrad, which is now Volgograd in Russia. He was 68 pounds and had tuberculosis and beriberi, a vitamin deficiency. It was too late to nurse him back to health. Another victim of the Holocaust."

"What about his sister, Rose?" Olivia asked.

"No one knows how or what she did to stay alive; she never spoke of it, not even to me. After the war, she found me in the U.S. through the United Jewish Welfare Fund."

"So she made it here. Are you still in touch? Did she marry and raise a family?" Olivia asked.

"The war damaged her," Ursula paused, as tears ran down both cheeks. She sized up her audience, then looked up to the ceiling to control her tears and said, "She married twice. Had four wonderful children. The family was living in the San Francisco Bay Area. One day she was driving over the train tracks near the airport. Her car stalled on the tracks. She couldn't get out in time, and was killed instantly when the train hit. At least that was the official story."

"The official story?" Reuben asked.

"Personally, I think it was survivor's guilt."

"Like some of our soldiers with PTSD?" Olivia said. "The ones who come back from Iraq and Afghanistan and think that they should have died instead of their friends?"

"Yes, darling. Like that."

"So even after all these years, after Hitler and his Nazis were long gone, they were still killing Jews and messing with their lives, huh?" Reuben asked.

"And others, too," Ursula said. "There was this young man named Leon who worked in a bookstore here in the States. He used to help me pick out books, I've always loved to read. Anyway, he took a long leave of absence from the store. When he returned, I asked him to coffee. He seemed so sad. He told me that his father had died, but there seemed to be more to it than that. I finally got him to tell me the whole story. He was so embarrassed, because he knew I was Jewish. But I found out that his father had been a guard at one of the forced-labor, concentration camps in Germany. He never personally killed anyone. But after the war, when he found out what had been going on in his camp and others, and that he was a part of it, he started to drink. He kept on drinking after he came to the U.S. until he finally drank himself to death. So he and his family were another casualty of the craziness that was the Nazis."

"His family too?" Olivia said.

"Of course dear. They ended up living with a drunk, which isn't easy. And then, they had to deal with his premature death and the disgrace of what he thought was just his service to his country."

Chapter 16

"Children," Ursula said to her teary-eyed audience. "I'm sorry, but I need go to the bathroom again, and then lie down for a few minutes. I think maybe I overdid it the past couple of days. Too much excitement. Too much burrito and *camarones*. But oh so good."

Both young people took their cues. Olivia dried her eyes on a paper napkin and rose to help Ursula to the bathroom. "Let me know when you're done in there, *abuela*. Don't try to get to the bedroom by yourself," she finished, thinking that she detected her new, old friend getting more frail right before her eyes. It must be from not taking her medications, the nurse-in-training projected. Somehow, she thought, she had to get Ursula to tell her what was ailing her, find out what prescriptions she needed, and get them for her.

As the women took the few steps toward the bathroom, Reuben cleaned off the table and started doing dishes. As he washed and stacked them to dry, Olivia leaned against the door frame with her coffee mug in both hands.

"Does she look like maybe she's getting weaker or something?"

"You know, now that you mention it, she's not as ah, you know, ah, peppy, as she was a couple of nights ago. She was kinda funny and having a good time after we left the clinic. I was pushing her in the wheelchair and it was like, ah, kinda like she was on a ride at Disneyland or something. Now she seems like an old lady. What's happening? Are we bringing her down with all this talk about Nazis and dead people?"

"Maybe. But, for some reason, it seems she wants to tell her story. Besides, it might be selfish, but I think it's really interesting. You know, I studied all that stuff in school. But to hear about from someone who was really there, it's like just reading about something and then getting to see the really cool 3-D movie that's been made from the book."

"Yeah, I know what you mean. So what could it be? Or is she just, you know, old old?"

"Well, she's definitely old. Didn't she say she was 87? That's just thirteen years from a hundred. That's pretty old."

"But, I think she would be doing better if she had her meds."

"Any ideas how we can find out where she lives so we can go get them, or something?" Reuben said.

"She obviously doesn't want to tell us, or she would have by now. She's a very strong-willed woman. You'd have to be to live through just the shit she's told us so far, and you know there's more to come. She keeps talking about Holland and Cuba," Olivia said.

"I can't even wrap my head around that. I mean, what? From tulips to sugar cane?" Reuben surprised Olivia with his knowledge of the flora that seemed to represent the two divergent cultures. "Man, and the way she speaks Spanish. I mean it's good and all, but her German accent, you don't hear that very much."

Olivia just had time to crack a smile at Reuben's comment about Ursula's Spanish. Then she heard the click of the bathroom door handle. She reached into the kitchen to put her mug on the counter and turned toward the bathroom to help Ursula to her grandmother's bedroom.

"*Gracias, niña.* I'm feeling better now. If you two would like, and you can make me a cup of tea, I'd rather continue my story. There's plenty of time to sleep later."

Olivia looked into the kitchen. Reuben shrugged.

"Okay, *abuela*," Olivia said. "Would you like to sit at the table, or maybe the sofa? Or the chair in the living room might be more comfortable?"

"I'll take the sofa," Ursula said. Without saying a word to each other, Olivia and Reuben changed places. He took Ursula by one arm, while putting the other around the woman's waist. Olivia went into the kitchen, filled a kettle and put it on the stove. She also filled two glasses with water and walked them out to the living room for Reuben and herself.

"Would you like some water, too?" she said to Ursula. "No thank you. Well, on second thought, it will take a few minutes for the tea. Yes, water would be nice," Ursula said as Reuben gently lowered her down to the sofa. As he turned to take his place in the chair opposite, he caught Olivia's eye as she went toward the kitchen. Just the smallest nod from him told her that he thought her suspicions about Ursula's declining condition were correct.

* * *

"Amsterdam was better by far than either Danzig or Königsberg," Ursula jumped right in where she had left off, taking just a moment to sip a little water. "Our apartment wasn't much larger than the tiny one we had in Danzig. But we felt we had the opportunity here to begin to rebuild our lives. The Dutch people were, and are, much more tolerant of people's religions and lifestyles. During the war years, from about 1939 to 1945, Jews in Germany, Poland and other countries were made to sew yellow Jewish stars, the Star of David, onto their clothes. This would let gentiles know who was a Jew, and make it easier to discriminate against them—deny them services, bully them and even physically abuse them. But in Holland, more than 300,000 yellow Stars of David were made and worn by the Dutch, Jew or Gentile, as a sign of solidarity.

"Of course, we had already left Holland by then, but I was so proud of my friends and neighbors there. In my mind, they are among the most righteous of the Righteous."

"What are the Righteous?" Reuben asked a nanosecond before Olivia could get the words out of her mouth.

"They are the Gentiles, businessmen and women, doctors, nurses, ordinary individuals, even some ministers and priests who helped protect Jews from the Nazis. Many even found ways to smuggle Jews out of Germany and other countries, or just helped them along the way, like that family in Berlin that took us in just before we left for Poland. They are the same people who would defend the weak and the minority in any country. But doing it in the face of certain incarceration in a concentration camp, and probably death, takes a heroic effort. Surprisingly, that's almost everyone who was living in Holland.

"However, having seen the Nazi cancer spread across Eastern Europe, and being aware of its supporters and followers in France, Spain, Italy and even England, my father wasn't content to just stay in Holland and wait to see what would happen. So he kept on trying to get us visas to the U.S.

"My mother had two half-sisters already living here. And both said they would sponsor the family; make sure we didn't end up on welfare, help us get settled and get jobs. But the Jewish quota kept us out. By that time, the State Department was actually becoming aware of the plight of Jews in Germany, Czechoslovakia and Poland. So, now they were giving preference to them. It was ironic. Because my father had done all that he could to save our family, we were now even further away from a visa than if we had stayed in Berlin. Although we criticized the policy and policy makers for not waking up to Hitler's threats earlier, we could not begrudge our Jewish 'cousins' whose lives were in greater peril, the benefit of moving to the head of the immigration line. For the time being, we were reasonably safe."

"It must have been tough moving from one country to another in just a few years," Olivia said.

"It was. We even moved a couple more times in Holland. But that was all right. We finally felt like human beings instead of some kind of hunted vermin. As always, Father took in clothes to mend, made some suits for wealthy clients, and put away as much money as he could so we would have passage to the U.S. when the time came. Actually, by this time, Father was considering other alternatives. He figured that if we couldn't get into the U.S., maybe we could immigrate to Canada or Mexico. Anywhere in the Western Hemisphere, just as far away from the coming storm in Europe as possible."

"Is that how you ended up in Cuba?" Reuben said.

"*Sí, niño*. Actually, father came home one day from standing in line at the U.S. Embassy in Amsterdam very excited. He told us a man had approached him and others with an opportunity to sail to Canada in a week. Canada, he thought. Why not? It's close to the U.S., they speak mostly English, which is not difficult for Germans to learn. They're democratic, part of the British Commonwealth, who were about the only country really standing up to Hitler at that time. It all sounded good.

"Father considered himself a shrewd man. He knew there were con men and thieves preying on Jews. Promising to get them to freedom, taking their money and disappearing. So," Ursula stopped to finally sip some tea and build some tension, "he told the man to show him the ship. He said he wanted to talk to the captain in person.

"The man took him right then down to the docks where a steamship with a Cuban flag was docked. There was no wind, so my father only saw the red, white and blue of the flag as it hung limp. He didn't know the Canadian flag is a red maple leaf on a white background, he just thought he was seeing a flag from a friendly country—which was true.

"Anyway, he didn't understand Spanish, but he heard the word Canada when the captain and the other man were talking. In retrospect, we think the man making the arrangements just threw that in so Father would hear it. Or maybe the ship was supposed to sail by Canada to get to Cuba.

"Again, being a shrewd man, my Father insisted on paying the captain of the ship and having him acknowledge that passage was paid. He also made sure that he understood when we were to leave and as many other details as he could glean. The captain, of course, took some of the money Father had given him and gave it to the other man, but that was to be expected.

"As you already know, the ship was never going to go to Canada. Without knowing it, we had booked passage to Cuba. But at least it was far away from the craziness in Europe. The passage over was mostly uneventful. We got caught in one heavy storm and every passenger on board got seasick, except me. I was alone in the galley eating with the crew, who were used to heavy seas. It was the first time I experienced Cuban cooking, and I loved it immediately. It's probably also why so many of the passengers had gotten so sick.

"The seas calmed down on October ninth. I remember the date because October tenth is my grandfather's *yahrtzeit*."

"What's a yard site?" Reuben said.

"It's pronounced *yahrtzeit*, honey. Hear the 'z'? *Yahrtzeit*."

"Okay, but what does it mean?"

"It is to remember the anniversary of a loved one's passing. At sundown the day before the anniversary of the passing of a loved one—which is actually the beginning of the new day in Jewish tradition—observant Jews and even non-observant Jews light a *yahrtzeit* candle that will burn for at least twenty-four hours."

"How many years do Jews do this?" Olivia said.

"As long as they want. Some do it for the rest of their lives. Others for only a few years. Whether you do it or not, doesn't mean you're not keeping their memory alive in your heart.

"Anyway, it was October ninth. The storm had passed, or we had passed through it. The waters were calm. My poor father was weak because he couldn't keep food down. He was dehydrated from being seasick, but he knew the date. 'We have to find a *yahrtzeit* candle,' was the first thing he said when he was beginning to feel well again."

"'Papa,' I told him, 'where will we find a *yahrtzeit* candle on a Cuban ship?' 'I don't know daughter, but it's your grandfather's *yahrtzeit* at sundown, you've got to find something.'

"So I went to talk with some of the members of the crew that I had eaten with while everyone else was sick. I knew they liked me because I was an 18-year-old girl. But also because I was eager to learn their language and I liked their food. As good Catholics, several had votive candles they would light for saints and loved ones. But they wouldn't burn for twenty-four hours. I managed to collect six of them, hoping each would last at least four hours. It meant staying up all night, or waking up in the middle of the night to make sure that one was always burning. I brought them to father. At first, he didn't understand. 'We're only commemorating my father's passing,' he said. 'Not all of our relatives.'

"I explained my plan to keep one burning at all times and he commended me for my thoughtfulness and ingenuity. It was one of the proudest moments of my life.

"At sundown, we lit the first candle under the watchful eyes of my loyal Cuban admirers. I sat in a chair reading or chatting with my brother as we stood watch. About four hours later, we lit the next one from the waning flame of the first candle. That one lasted almost five hours, but I didn't. I curled up on my little cot and fell asleep sometime after one in the morning. The candle would have gone out around two. Without my knowing it, whichever member of the crew was on duty made it a point to come by the room the whole family was sharing. They told me later that they would look under the door where they could see just my feet in the candle light as I sat in my chair. They hoped they could tell from the position and movement of my feet if I was still awake or had drifted off. Actually a little unnerving in retrospect. But it saved my grandfather's *yahrtzeit*.

"Apparently very quietly, again somewhat unnerving in retrospect, one of my gallant Cuban friends stole into our cabin and gently shook me awake. I almost screamed when I saw his face above me. But I didn't. I don't know if it was because I was suddenly aware of why he was there and what I needed to do, because he was holding a finger to his lips with one hand while he took the other off my shoulder and pointed to the still burning candle, or because, quite truthfully, he was a ruggedly handsome young man.

"Regardless, nobody else woke up. I up righted myself on my cot, got the next votive candle and held it sideways over the diminishing flame of the other candle. He slipped out the door as quietly as he had come in, never saying a word. It was already daylight by the time we had to light another candle."

"So you kept a candle burning for the whole yahrtz-whatsits?" Reuben said.

"Indeed we did."

"Whatever happened to the handsome Cuban?" Olivia said.

"I saw him a couple of days later. He and another member of the crew were sharing a cigarette on the bow of the ship. They were both facing out to sea, but so close together their hips were touching, you know what I mean, honey? Anyway, I walked up and thanked him in pretty good Spanish. Of course, I scared the hell out of them. That was when I was sure of what I was seeing. '*Señora, por favor* . . .' he implored me.

"'*No problema, mi amigo. Muchas gracias,*' I said."

Chapter 17

Ursula drank from her teacup and then put it back on the side table next to the couch. "It was only a few days later when we made port in Havana. It was good to be on dry land again. Since our ship was a freighter, there wasn't anyone on the docks to meet us, except some customs officers who were more interested in the ship's cargo than us. They quickly stamped our German passports with hardly a glance. Our little family of four hardly looked like anyone they needed to concern themselves with.

"By that time I had learned enough Spanish to find us a hotel and eventually a synagogue where we could meet other Jewish refugees and start another new life in another strange country.

"We had never experienced so much sunshine and humidity. Our skin was soft and moist, but we also sweated like pigs. Father got a job almost immediately in a shop that made those white, loose-fitting shirts that are so practical in Cuba's climate. The tourist trade was good, and lots of people who might normally travel to Europe were coming to the island for gambling and the nightlife. They would come down from New York and Chicago and, before they would die in their regular clothes, they would buy these shirts. Of course, the island people paid next to nothing for theirs, and the matching pants. But the tourists didn't know that, or where to get the cheap ones, so they bought from my father's employer, Saul. They were also more comfortable dealing with an American instead of a Cuban. So, they paid ten times as much, but that was cheap by U.S. standards.

"Saul hired me, too, to help with purchasing materials, since my Spanish was getting better by the day. Saul spoke Yiddish, as did almost every Jew then. And Yiddish has a lot in common with regular German, not the high German, but what most people spoke every day; just one more thing Hitler hated about Jews.

"Working with Saul, I started to learn English. And soon, I was helping to sell to customers. In the mornings, if I wasn't helping Saul to get materials from Cubans, I was helping father: cutting fabric, stitching on patch pockets, hemming the bottoms of the shirts. Mother couldn't get work cleaning because no one in the Cuba we knew could afford a housekeeper. So she started doing embroidery work on some of Saul's shirts, which would double their already inflated prices. But they sold well. People on vacation don't look at price tags as hard as they do at home. And everyone wanted a colorful souvenir of their stay on the island."

"What was your brother doing all this time?" Olivia said.

"Mostly playing with other children. He was supposed to be doing chores at home, but almost always found an excuse to avoid them. It was like he didn't want to know what was going on in the world. Which is ironic, because when we finally got to the U.S. and he was old enough, he enlisted in the army, and then made it his career."

"Where is he now?" Olivia asked.

"I think he's living in New York. We haven't spoken in years."

"Was there a fight or something?" Reuben asked.

"Well, if I can digress for a moment. I just got fed up with him about 20 years ago. He was one of those people who just sent everyone a copy of the same pompous letter at Christmas time telling them what wonderful escapades he had during the year. That he was at the same restaurant as this famous person or that, went to an art opening, Broadway play or something else where there were a lot of big shots. It was like fame and importance by association.

"Except for those braggadocio letters, and a very rare phone call, we hadn't seen each other in a dozen years. He was always too busy with important stuff to come to family functions, like my daughter's bat mitzvah and my son's bar mitzvah, or either of their weddings. Then, when our mother died, I tried to call him so he could come to the memorial. I left two messages to call me right away. I didn't want to leave a message that said, 'Our mother is dead.'"

Despite the macabre nature of Ursula's narrative, Reuben found himself stifling a laugh.

"Anyway, a few days later I got a letter from him that said, you won't believe this, but I memorized the damn thing, it bothered me so much, 'I imagine our mother is dying or dead. She is twenty-five years older than us, and I doubt I will reach her age. You and I split over Clinton, communist, enemy of Israel. Do you still support him? Best regards, Walter.'"

"Jesus," Olivia said. "What did you do then?"

"Nothing. I wouldn't dignify his arrogant little snipe with an answer."

"What happened then?" Reuben asked.

"Nothing. Really. Haven't heard from him since. Haven't tried to talk or write to him. Don't even know if he's still alive."

"Don't you wish you could just kill him?" Reuben said.

"No *niño*. That would give him too much power over me. It's bad enough I remember the letter word-for-word. But to put any more effort into the situation is just a waste of my time. He's not worth the effort it takes to hate. I'm completely indifferent to him. I really don't care if he wins a lottery or breaks a leg, he just isn't important enough for me to expend what little energy I have left over him."

"Well, I know that if I could ever find out who killed my brother Julian, I would make him pay for it."

"That's exactly what I mean. You need to forgive and move on. I'm not saying you should forget Julian and all the wonderful things he was. But don't waste the time you need to grow and learn and live by wishing someone else harm. Especially when you have no idea who that someone might be."

Reuben looked at Olivia for a moment. She looked back with compassion and understanding, but didn't say a word. Then he looked down at the carpet, noticing the intricate pattern woven into the fabric, how one lovely element flowed into another to form a most beautiful piece of art; and he understood what Ursula meant. "*Gracias, abuela*, I will try to remember that.

Olivia waited two beats, then gently said, "So you were learning English and Spanish and how to sew shirts, then what happened?"

Reuben looked back up at Ursula. She smiled, took another sip of tea and continued. "I didn't realize it, but I was learning a profession that would serve me for the rest of my life.

"I have to say, living in Cuba was a paradise compared to the hate and persecution that grew as the Nazis gained more power and became more influential. Cuba was a poor country then, as it is now. Most of the population was oppressed by the Batista regime, just like they have been oppressed by the Castro regime. It seems that some countries just can't get away from these self-serving bastards. Anyway, for us, the poverty wasn't nearly as bad as the persecution we would have experienced if we had stayed in Europe, though I have to say, things never got as bad in Holland as we feared. But enough about world history. This is about me, no?"

Reuben and Olivia smiled and applauded Ursula with a small chuckle.

"Father never stopped trying to get us visas to come to the U.S. He was on a first-name basis with the people at the U.S. Embassy in Havana. One woman in particular, Mrs. Krauss. I think her first name might have been Shirley. She was a fourth-generation American, descended from Austrian Jews who had actually fought in the American Revolution. Technically, she qualified to be a member of the D.A.R."

"What's the D.A.R.?" Olivia asked.

"Daughters of the American Revolution. It's open to any woman with good moral character who has proof that an ancestor fought the British in 1776. However, up until the 1950s or 1960s, it really wasn't open to Jews, Negros and other people of color. But that's beside the point. Things are getting better.

"Anyway. Mrs. Krauss may not have been in the D.A.R., but she was a kind person and a patriotic American. I think she kind of liked papa. Maybe he reminded her of someone she liked or loved. Regardless, she took a special interest in our family. She suggested a better part of town where there were nicer apartments that we could still afford. Things like that. She also kept an eye out for an opportunity to get us to the U.S. She watched the quotas for Jews, quotas for specific trades, quotas for Germans, quotas for Cubans—I guess she thought since we were living in Havana, that we could pass for Cuban—whatever she could think of. She knew we had sponsors here, so that put us ahead of other families. Finally, when the U.S. became the main resource for materials for the allies who were fighting the Germans, she managed to get us visas because my father was a tailor, and, supposedly, the U.S. needed trained garment workers to help sew uniforms and things for the allied forces. Little did we realize, that by the time we got to the U.S., just before Pearl Harbor, Father would become a manager in a factory making uniforms for U.S. troops.

"By the time our ship docked in New York—Florida would have been a lot closer, but that's the government for you, they wanted to process us in New York, not even Ellis Island—I was already 20 years old. We moved first to Chicago; that's where Father managed workers making army uniforms. It's also where I met my first husband. We were both taking English lessons in night school. He and his family had just recently immigrated from Hungary. We got married just before he got drafted and was sent for training at Fort MacArthur near Long Beach. That is how I first came to live in Southern California.

"It seemed like he had just enough time to come to the U.S., get married and become a citizen before the army shipped him back to Europe."

"So, he was a war hero?" Reuben asked.

"He spent a good deal of the war trying to stay alive. I mean, he fought and probably killed enemy soldiers, but he never talked about it afterwards. You could tell that it had a profound effect on him. I think it contributed to his skepticism politically and religiously."

"What do you mean?" Olivia asked.

"Well, he was never a very religious Jew, but after the war he seemed to become more of an atheist than anything else. He couldn't imagine a God that would make men like Hitler and Stalin, Mussolini and Tojo, or who would allow decent young men in all armies to become inhuman savages. He read a lot, and believed that, as he put it, 'religion was invented by the power elite to appease peasants for their crappy lives by promising them a wonderful, mythical future beyond the grave in exchange for their servitude in this life.'"

"Wow, so he didn't believe in God or heaven?" Reuben asked.

"What do you believe, Ursula?" Olivia asked.

"No, Reuben, he didn't believe in any of that. He thought religious leaders are just another type of oppressive overlord who are only interested in wealth and power.

"As for your question Olivia, I just don't know. I see merit in what Josef believed. But I've also seen religion help a lot of people in myriad ways. It might keep them from breaking laws, lying, cheating, taking drugs or just breaking down psychologically. So, for some, in some ways, it can help. Perhaps it is as Karl Marx said, 'Religion is the opiate of the masses.' But so what? Sometimes we all need a vacation, or a drink, or a drug, or just someone else to tell us that everything is going to be all right."

"You said he was skeptical about politicians, too?" Olivia said.

"He lumped them all together. He said politicians were just power hungry despots who wanted to gild their nests—that is, get as much as they can for themselves. But he thought the same for dictators, kings, kaisers, czars, presidents, popes and other

84

religious leaders. I'll grant him this: he thought many who actually worked in government and church outreach were gracious and caring people who really made a difference for those in need. But he thought that they, too, were being taken advantage of by the establishments for which they worked."

"It sounds like he was hard to live with?" Olivia said.

"He was."

"What happened to him?" Reuben asked.

"He passed away a few years ago. He wasn't feeling well and his doctor sent him to the hospital. The next day he died peacefully. He was on his third wife. I'm told she looked a lot like I did when I was fifty," Ursula laughed.

"And you?" Olivia asked.

"And me? I'm tired."

"Should I take you into the bedroom?"

"No, no. Why don't you kids go get some lunch or go shopping or something. Just let me lie down here for an hour. You need to get out in the sun, I'll be fine."

Chapter 18

"Richard," Deborah Frank Samuel said to her husband. "We've got to do something. The police haven't gotten any information about Mom. I don't think they've done a damn thing. And, Mike isn't answering his phone."

I can't really blame him, Richard Samuel thought to himself, I wouldn't answer my phone either if it was the tenth call in three hours from my hysterical sister. However, while that was what Richard was thinking, he said, "Deborah, I'm sure the police are doing everything they can. And Mike's probably just in a dead cell phone area," —a near impossibility in Southern California. Richard and Deborah hadn't used the diminutive of their given names, Dick and Debbi, since they became movie set caterers nearly twenty years earlier, and then joined the country club set five years later. They hadn't made a sandwich for their business, or their children, since then. Instead, they ran crews of chefs, servers, bussers and dishwashers on as many as five film sets at a time.

* * *

"Mike," his girlfriend Joyce said, "why don't you answer your phone?"

"It's just Debbi freaking out for the umpteenth time," he answered. Mike *always* used the diminutive of his sister's name. As much because it was what he called her while they were growing up, and well into adulthood, as it was to remind her that she was just another little Jewish girl from the Valley.

"Then that's all the more reason you should talk to her. Maybe you can calm her down," she said, as Mike finally found a parking space in the Lilliputian parking lot of a Trader Joe's.

"That's very sweet of you to care so much about her, but believe me, there's nothing I can do about my mother or my sister right now. I'm concerned about Mom. I hope she's okay and that the police or someone finds her soon, but I don't know what I can possibly do for her at the moment. As for my sister, I'm pretty sure she's happy being miserable about Mom, and about not being able to talk at me about her."

"You make Debbi sound like a masochist."

"In some ways, I think she is."

"But there must be something we can do to help."

86

"You tell me what that is, and I'm all over it," he said as they got out of his BMW to do a little grocery shopping. He was also running low on wine at the condo, but he thought getting anything more than the bare essentials was kind of callous, under the circumstances. He really did want his mother to be all right. And he really would have done something more to find her, but he was just a bit tharn about the whole incident. It was totally new territory and he hadn't the slightest idea how to act or react. He just kept silently repeating a little prayer to himself that Ursula would be found soon, unharmed.

* * *

Officers Gallagher and Swarzen were indeed doing all they could do in the Valley. They had talked with many shopkeepers in the area of the assisted living facility where Ursula lived. Although a few actually recognized her, none had seen her recently. They also took on the thankless job of getting out of their squad car and walking down and around in the washes nearby, thankfully finding nothing more interesting than the usual assortment of trash—from old tires and appliances to yards of worn carpet and enough lumber for Habitat for Humanity to build a small village.

They walked through the parks in the area looking under bushes and hoping not to find a decaying body that someone had stashed there. Although they disturbed several homeless people and discovered a stash of beer and condoms deep inside a cavernous clearing in some bushes, they found no evidence of any missing persons.

* * *

The mid-town L.A.P.D. officers, Lincoln and Pascal, had turned over their grand-theft auto suspect, Marco Lopez, to the district attorney. Their case was good. Fingerprints on the stolen Toyota, positive I.D., known gang member; it was a slam dunk.

They knew the kid should go to prison—he was old enough to be considered an adult—but they also realized that their case was so good, the D.A. would leverage Marco for a bigger bust and let the kid plead to a lesser charge; one that would probably get him parole instead of hard time. They didn't harbor any illusions of Marco actually rehabilitating himself, but there was always hope.

Chapter 19

Once outside the apartment building, Reuben said to Olivia, "I'm worried about her. She seemed so happy and lively just a couple of days ago."

"She needs her medications," Olivia answered.

"So we need to stop letting her talk to us about her life before and get her to talk about who she is now. What kinda sickness, or whatever she has, so we can get her some pills or something."

"I know, I know. I've been listening closely but she hasn't given up any information. We know she has children and has been married more than once. But she's not giving us anything to go on," Olivia said as they made their way aimlessly up the street. "I even went through that little purse she has for some I.D., or a bottle of pills. But there's nothing in there except a few tissues and old wrapped candy mints, probably left over from the last time she ever went out for an evening. I think the only thing we can do is confront her. Tell her straight out that we need to know who she is and where she lives, or she might be in great danger soon because she hasn't had her meds for days. That could make her very sick and in pain. Depending on what medical problems she has, it might even kill her."

"Well, you're the nurse."

"In training."

"But you know a hell of a lot more than I do. And you're a woman. You guys should bond."

Olivia let the juxtaposition of 'woman' and 'guys' slide as she beamed inwardly at the mention of her being a woman. "Okay. This is what we should do. Let's grab a sandwich or something at the *bodega* around the corner. We can get a tuna salad, or something else for Ursula that'll be easy on her stomach. We can eat our lunch on the steps, that should give her an hour or so to rest. Then we'll go back upstairs and tell her that she has to tell us where she lives so we can get her back and get her the care she needs."

"Let's give it a shot. She's pretty damn strong-willed, but you're right, we've got to do something. Besides, I've got to be back in school Monday."

"Yeah, and I have to get back to work and nursing school. I'm sure if we tell her that, she'll give in. She's gotta."

* * *

Olivia and Reuben finished off their sandwiches, some chips and a couple of sodas, and then took a chicken salad sandwich that looked fresher than the tuna at the *bodega* up to Ursula. When they entered the apartment the older woman was still lying on the couch. Soft, sleepy snores were coming from her mouth, which hung open in a most unflattering manner.

"*Abuela*," Olivia said as she gently nudged her shoulder. Reuben had gone into the kitchen to put the sandwich on a plate and get a glass of cold water for their charge.

"Ooog," came the older woman's reply. Then, "Oh, you're back already. What's your rush, you just left."

"Ursula," Olivia said as Reuben came back into the living room, a plate in one hand, a glass in the other. "We've been gone over an hour. I'm glad you had a chance to rest. We brought you a sandwich, it's chicken salad, is that all right?"

"I'm not hungry, child. But hand me that water." She drank down a third of the glass, a good sign, Olivia thought.

"Listen, Ursula," Olivia continued, trying to sound final but friendly, "you have to tell us who you really are and where you live. You've been without any medication for at least half a week. I know you have a serious condition, you could be jeopardizing your life."

"I know dear. You don't get to be my age and see as many doctors and have as many tests done as I have and not know that."

"So why wouldn't you want to take better care of yourself?" Reuben asked.

"I was working my way up to that," Ursula said. "I wouldn't have told you a thing about me if I didn't think that somehow my story might help you," she looked directly at Reuben, "and even you," she turned her look of motherly compassion on Olivia.

"You see," she went on before either of them could formulate another question or demand, "at first, I came down to this part of L.A. with the hope of getting seriously mugged. I've had a pretty good life since arriving in the United States, at least until my children convinced me to move here from Arizona.

"My late husband Bernie and I lived there for nearly twenty years. We had friends our age, though lots of them are dying off at an alarming rate—that's what happens at my age. But there are still enough left that I had company that I felt comfortable with.

89

"But my kids, well, at least my daughter, wanted me to move, so she and her kids could spend more time with me. Kind of pack in as much as possible before the old lady kicked the bucket."

Both Olivia and Reuben jerked back as if they had been smacked in the chest with bean bags.

"Don't be so shocked," Ursula continued. "We're all going to die sometime. Hopefully while we still have some steam left in us so we can go with dignity. The last thing I want is to be wired up like a puppet waiting for someone with enough compassion, consideration and guts to cut me loose. To set my soul, such as it may be, free."

"So you believe in the soul?" Olivia asked.

"Oh, I don't know dear. How can anyone who isn't dead know about such things? But what does it matter? If it's there, then just set it free. If there isn't any soul—and there certainly isn't a gram of scientific evidence to say there is—then just set *me* free. Free from pain, free from not being able to eat what I want, free from the confines of a body that just doesn't work the way it used to. Is that too much to ask?"

"I guess not," Olivia mumbled at the floor. Reuben just looked on surprised. He didn't want to hear that there may *not* be a soul. He didn't want to hear that his brother Julian was just gone. Gone forever. Nothing. Like trying to understand the meaning of zero and why it is so important. Reuben wanted Julian to be there somehow. He wanted his brother to be somewhere where he could watch over him. But, if Julian's soul was watching over Reuben, why didn't he stop him from trying to steal that car? Where was it when Marco, like Satan himself, convinced Reuben to join the *Diecinueves*?

Or was it there? Did Julian somehow send Ursula to downtown L.A. to come between him and the *Diecinueves*? Maybe that was it. Maybe Julian *was* watching over him. He wished there was a way to know. He wanted to ask Ursula to find out after she died. To somehow give him a sign. Words on a foggy mirror that only he would see, and then vanish like fog blowing out to sea. But he was afraid to ask her. He didn't think it would be polite to remind someone that they are so close to dying.

"So, what happened?" Olivia broke into Reuben's thoughts.

"Well, about moving here," Ursula continued, "my children and their children didn't live up to their promise of spending more

90

time with me. I don't really blame them, they have their lives, what would they want with an old lady?

"So, I just felt stuck here. Made some new friends, but I was so much happier back in Arizona."

"Why not move back?" Reuben asked.

"At my age? Just getting to the mall on the home's shuttle bus takes half a day and all my energy. If I had tried to go back to Arizona I would have been dead before I got to San Bernardino. I felt trapped for the first time since I arrived in the U.S. Which, by the way, I still need to finish telling you about."

"Not another word about your life until you tell us your real name and where you live," Olivia said.

"I told you my real name, it's Ursula."

"Ursula what?"

The older woman paused, then said, "If you let me wrap this up fast, I'll tell you what you want to hear, as well as what I think you need to hear."

This time, Olivia hesitated. Reuben looked on as the two women horse-traded as well as any man he had ever seen. "Okay," the nurse-in-training finally said. "But first, tell us your full name, just as a sign of good faith."

"Oh dear, you do take yourself so seriously. You must learn to laugh more and enjoy life. 'Angels can fly because they take themselves lightly.' Of course, I've been married twice, but my legal name now is Ursula Frank."

"Like Ann Frank?" Olivia asked in surprise.

"Yes, but no relation," she took another sip of water.

"And where do you live, Ursula Frank?" Olivia said.

"Hand me my purse dear."

"But there's nothing in it but tissues and candy."

"And you shouldn't be looking through other people's private business," Ursula said making Olivia blush with shame. When she was given the purse, Ursula reached under the couch cushion next to the one on which she was seated, pulled out a folded piece of paper and placed it in the purse. "I figured you would search my purse when I finally nodded off, so I put this under the cushion when we first arrived.

"As hopeless as it may sound, my wish was for some thug or gang member to knock me out—quick and nearly painless, like pulling off a Band-Aid. I'm old and frail, I thought a good clock to the noggin would kill me. Then the police, or whomever, would find my body and find the information they needed in my purse to notify the home and my children. That would be that.

"Instead, your gang," she looked at Reuben, "ignored me. And then I came around that corner and saw you and that other boy trying to steal that car. I thought maybe, if I tried to stop you, you or he would knock me out. It almost worked, too."

"Except you're too hard-headed to die from just hitting your head," Olivia said with a laugh.

"I guess so. And Reuben is just too nice a young man to just leave an old lady in the street. That's why I wanted to tell you about my life. See, I know it's not easy being a person of color in this country. It's something like being a Jew in Europe when the Nazis were coming to power. But, it's never really the same. My headache can never be as bad or as painful as yours is to you, that's just the way it is. It takes an enormous amount of compassion to realize someone else's pain. Most of us don't ever achieve that until something actually happens to us, or to a loved one.

"It's like the Reagan family's support of stem-cell research only after the former president was diagnosed with Alzheimer's, or the Cheney family's refusal to ostracize homosexuals because one of their daughters is gay—it just seems like, for most people, it has to directly affect them before they will give a tinker's damn about something.

"Sorry to get preachy, but you showed so much goodness on the street the other night, I wanted to try to give you back something.

"You know, even though we finally made it to the U.S., it wasn't always easy. In the 1950s and even into the 1960s there was anti-Semitism, but at least there weren't brown-shirted goons rounding us up to go to concentration camps to be murdered. Things got better. My first husband, who wanted to be a doctor when he was a boy in Hungary, became a very successful house painter. I took what I had learned from my father the tailor, and from embroidering and finishing shirts in Havana, and became a women's clothing designer.

"What I'm saying is, we didn't need to be bankers, lawyers and doctors, movie stars, CEOs or company presidents to be happy. We just needed to find a niche where our abilities and contributions would be appreciated. Where good honest work would pay a decent wage so we would have some dignity and be moderately comfortable.

"We didn't need a huge house, an expensive car or lots of fancy jewelry to be happy. In fact, most of that stuff won't keep you happy for long. Happiness comes from within, from feeling your self-worth. I think that the gardener at the home is happier than the CEO of the company that owns the place. When you see the gardener with his blooming plants and sensuous landscape, you can see how much he enjoys their beauty and how good he feels about the care and creativity he contributes to making the home a nicer place to be.

"The CEO's job is to make sure the place is making money. So what? You can't look at a pile of money and say you created it. You can spend it on things, but how many houses, cars and toys does it take to make you feel fulfilled? Do you realize that any king or queen from any time in history before the twentieth century would probably have traded their throne for what we consider an average lifestyle. They lived in drafty, dank castles, we live in well-heated, well-lit houses that keep out the wind and the weather. They had to shit in the woods, or in a bowl they kept under the bed, we have toilets. They had to bring water from a well or stream that was full of nasty microbes, we have hot and cold running water only steps away from wherever we're sitting or sleeping. They slept on straw, we have inner-spring mattresses, water beds, air beds, foam beds. They ate whatever was in season, we have fresh vegetables, fruit and meat whenever we want it. We are truly richer than any monarch, despot, pope, president or emperor that ever lived before the twentieth century.

"Don't blow it kids. You're both off to good starts. Olivia, you couldn't do better than to become a nurse, if that is your choice. You'll make a good living and help people at the same time. Reuben, you better keep your nose clean from now on. The police now have your fingerprints on file. The fact that they haven't been looking for you at your mother's house is a testament to you as having been a good boy, so far, because they haven't been able to match those prints to you or a previous crime. But the next time those prints show up somewhere . . ."

Reuben fidgeted in his seat, she really has been around, he thought.

"Anyway, you have talent with your hands and your mind. You might become an auto or airplane mechanic. High-demand jobs with good pay. If you work on your grades, you might become an engineer, if that is what you want."

"But, what if I try something like that and then I don't like it?" Reuben asked.

"Honey, you're young. You may not feel like it, but you are. If 'A' doesn't work out, try 'B' or 'C'. You're what? Eighteen? You'll have at least four more 18s before you're my age. When you consider that the first twelve years was just getting you ready for the big play, you'll have even more opportunities to find something with which you'll be happy," she drank more water, and leaned back into the couch. She looked up and closed her eyes.

"Go ahead and open the purse, Olivia."

Chapter 20

Deborah's cell phone rang and echoed off the granite counter of her hillside home. She leaped across the kitchen, grabbed the small device and checked the caller I.D.: Olivia Carillo.

Who the fuck is Olivia Carillo? she thought. It wasn't the assisted living home, that would have come up with the facility's name. Similarly, it wasn't the police. And it certainly wasn't her brother or any of her friends. And, since it was an election year, she figured it was just some political phone bank calling with a beg-and-plead for their candidate; so she pressed the "Ignore" key and slipped the annoying phone into the pocket of her DKNY slacks.

When Mike's cell phone rang in his pocket, he didn't even take it out to see that there was a call coming from Olivia Carillo, he just assumed that it was his hysterical sister again, and let it play out.

* * *

"*Abuela*," Olivia said softly to Ursula Frank, who was lying down on the short couch in the living room. "Deborah and Mike aren't answering. They won't be able to come to pick you up. Will you please let me drive you home?"

"You've done so much for me."

"It's all right. Reuben will come along."

"*Sí abuela, es me gusto*," Reuben said, hoping to give her comfort by speaking Spanish.

"Can you take me to the bathroom again?"

"Of course. Then we'll go. I'll call the home and let them know we're coming."

* * *

"Anna called from the home. Call me." Deborah texted to her brother from her cell phone.

At his girlfriend Joyce's urging, Mike looked at the message on his cell phone. "Who the fuck is Anna? And what home?"

"She's the caregiver at your Mom's assisted living home," Joyce said.

"Oh shit. How could I forget. Thanks," he said with genuine embarrassment. Then he called his sister. The call was brief. Deborah told him that some people were bringing their mother back to the home and would be there within the hour.

* * *

When Olivia and Reuben parked in front of the assisted living facility, two orderlies came through the double glass doors with a wheelchair. They expertly lifted Ursula from the front passenger seat of Olivia's Toyota Corolla and placed her gently in the chair. Deborah and Mike were right there asking their fatigued mother where had she been? What did she think she was doing? Telling her they were scared stiff. Demanding to know who the people with her were? Asking if they needed to call the police.

"Quiet," the older woman said, barely above a whisper.

"What?" Deborah said, "What Mom? Speak up, I can't hear you."

Ursula raised her right hand to her face and held her index finger in front of her mouth, the universal sign of all mothers for their kids to shut up. Everyone leaned in. "Dish ish Olibia and Reuben. Dey have been bery kind to me," Ursula said out of the right side of her mouth. "Be nice to dem. Dey will tell you eberyting."

"Mom, Mom, I don't understand what you're saying," Deborah said in a panic.

One of the men from the home asked Ursula if she could smile, and the older woman forced the muscles on the right side of her face to curl up. But the left side remained straight, even turning slightly down.

"Can you raise both of your arms?" he asked. And her right hand went up while her left remained lifeless in her lap. "You're having a stroke," he said. "We're going to call an ambulance right now," and he reached for the cell phone in the holster on his belt.

As the red and white van came speeding up the other side of the street and made a giant U-turn in front of the home, lights blinking, sirens screaming, Ursula reached her good right hand up and grabbed Reuben's hand. Olivia saw the gesture and both she and Reuben looked down at their friend. Their *abuela*, looked up, the right corner of her mouth turned up in a smile, the mischievous sparkle lighted up both of her eyes. Then her hand fell limp, her head lolled to one side, and she was at peace.

96

Chapter 21

Deborah, Mike, Reuben and Olivia all crouched down beside the lifeless woman in the wheelchair. Tears ran down the cheeks of them all. Individual thoughts ran rapid-fire through their heads: Ursula's/Mom's/*abuela's* incredible strength and understanding. Her perception, guidance and unequivocal love swept through each of them like warm brandy flowing through every artery, vein and capillary of their bodies.

One of the orderlies went over to talk with the ambulance drivers, to tell them there was no longer any urgency and to please give the family and friends a few more moments with their loved one. The other orderly went inside the assisted living home to let them know what had just happened. When he returned, he quietly told the ambulance drivers that Ursula Frank was a member of the Neptune Society and their services would not be needed.

The ambulance left. The orderlies told the quartet surrounding Ursula Frank that they needed to take her back into the home and up to her room, but that they were welcome to accompany them.

Together, they all walked into the lobby, but when the elevator arrived, Deborah said, "I think maybe the four of us need to talk." Everyone nodded. "We'll come back up in a few minutes."

Deborah, Mike, Reuben and Olivia found a quiet table in the far corner of the dining room of the home, away from the coffee urns and the few people that were there at the time. In hushed voices, Olivia and Reuben told Deborah and Mike about the last four days of their mother's life, omitting several details such as Reuben trying to steal a car and any mention of gangs.

They told the brother and sister duo that they did not know how or why Ursula came to be in the downtown area. Only that Reuben saw her on the street where she had either tripped and fallen or had barely managed to escape being mugged—a story that was all-to-plausible to a couple of white, upper-middle-class individuals from the Valley. Anyway, Reuben took her to the clinic where Olivia worked to get patched up, but she must have been suffering from some kind of amnesia until just this morning. They told Deborah and Mike about how Ursula seemed to be able to remember her entire life, but not her full name. They also told them that this morning she remembered how much she loved her children and wanted to be with them.

Olivia could see Deborah's and Mike's tension relieved as their shoulders relaxed and they sat up straighter. Meanwhile Reuben thought about what *abuela* had told him, "If you're going to lie, make sure there is enough truth in it to be credible."

"You two have been so kind to help someone you didn't even know," Deborah said, reaching for her purse, "can we give you a reward, or at least pay you back for your expenses?" she said, flipping the catch on her Coach purse and pulling out her wallet.

Reuben and Olivia looked at each other and read each other's thoughts, "No thank you," Olivia said. "Your mother has given us much more than we gave her."

"Isn't there anything we can do?" Deborah insisted.

"There is one thing. In her stories, your mother mentioned a special kind of candle that gets burned on the anniversary of a person's passing," Olivia said. "Do you know where we can get one?"

"You can find them at almost any supermarket around here," Mike said, trying to show his appreciation.

"Thank you," Olivia said.

"Can I ask why you want one?" Deborah asked.

"It's for Ursula's *yahrtzeit*," Reuben said.

Author's Note

I hope you have, or will, enjoy reading *Ursula's Yahrtzeit Candle*. If you belong to a book club whose members would enjoy a discussion with an author, I will gladly arrange a mutually convenient time to visit by phone, Skype, FaceTime, etc. You may contact me through my web site at http://www.StevenRBerger.com.

For more tidbits and information on *Ursula's Yahrtzeit Candle* and projects in the works, please visit http://www.StevenRBerger.com.

Thank you.